Trespassers Beware

"How many more are there, Ed?"

"Two or three. It's . . . hard to tell."

Before Slocum could wonder how someone could lose count of men who had taken a run at them while in the open, he felt a dizziness that sent a shiver through his eyeballs. The harder he tried to focus, the more difficult that simple task became. The leaves attached to the closest attacker fluttered and twisted in a breeze that wasn't there. One second, the figure seemed to be hunching down and leaning to the left, and the next, it was swaying to the right.

Another figure walked forward, carrying a staff with what looked to be a small animal's head on top of it. The dirty, blurry figures formed a crude circle around this one and became still when the gruesome staff was lifted high.

"Who are you?" Slocum wheezed. When he didn't get a response, he shouted, "Why did you attack us?"

"You, white men," the one with the staff said, "are trespassers."

"This is open territory," Slocum said.

"*No!* This ground is sacred. You insult it with the imprint of your wicked bodies. You scar it with the wheels of your wagons."

"We're on our way into Colorado," Ed insisted. "We're not going to harm anyone and never had any intention of settling anywhere near here."

"That is what all white men say. You will turn your wagons around and leave. *Leave*," the earthen figure said, "or *die*."

And then, like hazy mirages, the figures crouched down and disappeared.

DON'T MISS THESE
ALL-ACTION WESTERN SERIES
FROM THE BERKLEY PUBLISHING GROUP

THE GUNSMITH by J. R. Roberts

Clint Adams was a legend among lawmen, outlaws, and ladies. They called him . . . the Gunsmith.

LONGARM by Tabor Evans

The popular long-running series about Deputy U.S. Marshal Custis Long—his life, his loves, his fight for justice.

SLOCUM by Jake Logan

Today's longest-running action Western. John Slocum rides a deadly trail of hot blood and cold steel.

BUSHWHACKERS by B. J. Lanagan

An action-packed series by the creators of Longarm! The rousing adventures of the most brutal gang of cutthroats ever assembled—Quantrill's Raiders.

DIAMONDBACK by Guy Brewer

Dex Yancey is Diamondback, a Southern gentleman turned con man when his brother cheats him out of the family fortune. Ladies love him. Gamblers hate him. But nobody pulls one over on Dex . . .

WILDGUN by Jack Hanson

The blazing adventures of mountain man Will Barlow—from the creators of Longarm!

TEXAS TRACKER by Tom Calhoun

J.T. Law: the most relentless—and dangerous—manhunter in all Texas. Where sheriffs and posses fail, he's the best man to bring in the most vicious outlaws—for a price.

JAKE LOGAN

SLOCUM AND THE SPIRIT BEAR

J

JOVE BOOKS, NEW YORK

THE BERKLEY PUBLISHING GROUP
Published by the Penguin Group
Penguin Group (USA) Inc.
375 Hudson Street, New York, New York 10014, USA

Penguin Group (Canada), 90 Eglinton Avenue East, Suite 700, Toronto, Ontario M4P 2Y3, Canada (a division of Pearson Penguin Canada Inc.) • Penguin Books Ltd., 80 Strand, London WC2R 0RL, England • Penguin Group Ireland, 25 St. Stephen's Green, Dublin 2, Ireland (a division of Penguin Books Ltd.) • Penguin Group (Australia), 250 Camberwell Road, Camberwell, Victoria 3124, Australia (a division of Pearson Australia Group Pty. Ltd.) • Penguin Books India Pvt. Ltd., 11 Community Centre, Panchsheel Park, New Delhi—110 017, India • Penguin Group (NZ), 67 Apollo Drive, Rosedale, Auckland 0632, New Zealand (a division of Pearson New Zealand Ltd.) • Penguin Books (South Africa) (Pty.) Ltd., 24 Sturdee Avenue, Rosebank, Johannesburg 2196, South Africa

Penguin Books Ltd., Registered Offices: 80 Strand, London WC2R 0RL, England

This is a work of fiction. Names, characters, places, and incidents either are the product of the author's imagination or are used fictitiously, and any resemblance to actual persons, living or dead, business establishments, events, or locales is entirely coincidental.

SLOCUM AND THE SPIRIT BEAR

A Jove Book / published by arrangement with the author

PUBLISHING HISTORY
Jove edition / January 2013

Copyright © 2012 by Penguin Group (USA) Inc.
Cover illustration by Sergio Giovine.

ISBN: 978-0-515-15128-2

JOVE®
Jove Books are published by The Berkley Publishing Group, a division of Penguin Group (USA) Inc., 375 Hudson Street, New York, New York 10014. JOVE® is a registered trademark of Penguin Group (USA) Inc. The "J" design is a trademark of Penguin Group (USA) Inc.

PRINTED IN THE UNITED STATES OF AMERICA

10 9 8 7 6 5 4 3 2 1

ALWAYS LEARNING　　　　　　　　　　　　　　　　**PEARSON**

1

It was unseasonably cold for late October. The ground was hardened and dirtied by travelers heading west, and the trail they'd used was nothing more than a set of straight ruts in the ground. Countless wagons made the treacherous journey through Indian territory in the hopes of reaching lands more fertile or towns more prosperous than the ones they'd left behind. On all sides the ground was flat; beaten down by the elements and battered by a wind that never grew tired of tearing through dead stalks of wheat and corn. The most recent folks to brave the passage did so in a group of wagons lumbering westward through the howling winds.

When the group had left Springfield, Illinois, there were six wagons in the train. A fire set during a particularly brutal robbery outside of an unruly town in eastern Iowa forced them to leave one of the wagons behind like so many of the grave markers along the trails leading to California. Because so many of their possessions had been taken or burned, it wasn't difficult to consolidate what was left into the wagons that remained. If a sheriff and his deputies hadn't seen the flames from that wagon, the entire group could very well have been lost. But the lawmen came and chased away those robbers, allowing the wagon train to move along after burying their dead.

Foremost on the minds of the adults within those wagons was hiring on some protection. Josiah Pincher was handy with a rifle and had served some time in the Army, but one gunman in the group hadn't been enough to keep the bandits away, and when a nervous vote had been cast to look for another protector to accompany them, he didn't protest. They'd found a few likely prospects in some towns they'd visited, but none that were willing to travel with them all the way to the Rocky Mountains or were capable enough to do them much good if he did.

So, the wagons rolled the rest of the way through Iowa, flinching at every other rider they passed and praying their meager funds would see them all the way to their destination. The man who drove the lead wagon was Ed Warren; a tall fellow with broad shoulders and a wide face partially obscured by a thick, brushy beard. Narrow eyes set close together above a bulbous nose watched the trail for dangers and the skies for storms. A day's ride outside of Omaha, Ed parted ways with the wagons so he could ride down to Saint Joseph, Missouri, to see about calling in some favors that might be valuable enough to keep the wagons rolling. After his limited experience with hiring someone strictly for protection, he'd come to realize that many of the men best suited for the job were as much of a danger as those that might be chased away.

Ed's purpose for being in Saint Joseph was to call in a debt owed to him by an old business partner. As luck would have it, that partner was not only still in town, but still held Ed in high regard and was doing well enough to pay him back. Restitution was made in the form of a small bag of silver nuggets, a short stack of dollar bills, and a pair of solid gold cuff links. Eager to rejoin his wagons, Ed made his way to a general store closest to the edge of town to see what exhilarating pace that got steam coming from the horse's nostrils before it was asked to slow down.

Late in the afternoon, Ed sat at his place in the driver's seat of the lead wagon. Waving to Slocum, he asked, "See anything we need to worry about out there?"

"Not unless you're worried about falling asleep. Just a whole lot of wide-open country."

"That's what I like to hear! Keep up the great work, John."

Slocum's horse was standing in place, allowing the wagons to roll past it, which allowed him to hear Josiah when he grumbled, "Ain't like he made the damn country so flat."

Once the last wagon was rolling by, Slocum flicked his reins to get his horse moving again. He easily kept pace with Josiah while looking over to find the older man hunched forward as if he was studying every motion of his team's backside. "You got some quarrel with me?" Slocum asked.

"You know damn well how I feel. I never wanted you along for this ride and it looks more and more like there ain't no reason for you to be here."

"I've been doing everything that's asked of me."

"Sure," he chuckled. "I just bet you have."

Slocum couldn't be sure if Josiah's gaze had drifted toward Theresa's wagon in particular or if that was just his own suspicions tainting his thoughts. "What's that supposed to mean?"

"I don't gotta explain myself to nobody. Sure as hell don't gotta explain nothing to the likes of you."

Whatever Josiah knew about Theresa no longer mattered to Slocum. "You have a problem, then spit it out," he said. "Unless you'd rather just keep your head down and mumble like an old woman?"

Josiah's eyebrows rose and his upper body followed. In fact, it seemed as if he might stand up right there in the driver's seat to challenge Slocum when he replied, "Old woman? You sure you want to test your luck with me, boy?"

"Then hand over the money you got from in that store. I'll take anything else you got as well."

In the days following the attack that had resulted in the loss of one of his wagons as well as two of the souls who'd traveled with him, Ed had longed for an opportunity to stare those murdering sons of bitches in the eye. Throughout the search for another gun hand to ride with him, Ed had pondered the notion of doing the job himself just so he could get a chance to put a bullet into anyone else who might try to bring harm to the people who looked to him for guidance. Now that he was presented with such an opportunity, he wasn't about to let it pass.

Ed went for his gun. His finger barely scraped along the cold iron beside the trigger when he found himself looking down the barrel of a pistol held in the stranger's unwavering grip.

"Hand it over, mister," the stranger growled. "All of it. Right now, or I'll kill you and take it anyway."

Ed was weighing his options when another stranger lunged into view like a hawk swooping down to snatch an unsuspecting rodent from a canyon floor. The second stranger grabbed the first one's wrist and twisted until a pained grimace was written across the robber's face. Although the pistol was still mostly pointed at Ed, the man holding it didn't seem to be in any condition to pull the trigger.

"Best drop the smoke wagon before your wrist snaps," the new arrival warned.

The robber winced and let go, allowing his pistol to fall no more than a few inches before it was snatched from the air by the man who'd come along. Glaring through a hateful mask, the robber looked over to the new arrival and said, "This ain't none of your affair, Slocum."

"I told you to get out of town a few days ago, Vaccaro," the man named Slocum replied. "You're still here. The fact that you're trying to steal right out in the open so soon after

I had words with you means you're trying to make a fool out of me. I take that sort of thing very personal."

Vaccaro showed Slocum a shaky grin while trying to force his arm out of the other man's steely grasp. Unable to reclaim his hand, Vaccaro said, "Fine, then. I'll leave."

"You said that before."

"Well, now I know better. Ain't as if I can leave with you holding on to me like this."

When Slocum released Vaccaro's wrist, his fingers moved like the jaws of a steel trap. Cool eyes darted toward Ed just long enough to take the other man's stock. "Put your gun away, mister," he said. "You won't be needing it."

Since he'd barely moved it within its holster, Ed eased it back into place and kept his hand on the grip so he could skin the weapon if the need arose.

Vaccaro stepped back a few paces and squared his shoulders to the men in front of him. "Guess I'll be on my way, huh, Slocum?"

"Yeah."

"No hard feelings?"

After a few tense moments, Slocum shrugged. "I suppose not. It's not like you hurt this man."

"Right!" Vaccaro said through a sloppy grin filled with rust brown teeth. "A man's gotta earn his keep one way or another. Some of us are just wayward, is all. I'll move along and do better in the next town."

"Sure you will. Here," Slocum said while tossing the gun he'd taken. "Can't leave you at the mercy of whatever you might find between here and wherever you're going."

Vaccaro caught the pistol awkwardly, tossing it from one hand to another as if it were a piece of bread that had been pulled straight from the oven. Eventually, he got his hand around its grip. Judging by the look on his face, he was even more surprised than Ed that the pistol had been returned.

"Get out of my sight," Slocum said. "If I see you again, you won't live long enough to regret it."

Ed dared not move. When his horse shifted beneath him, he felt as if he'd reintroduced himself to the killers who'd forgotten he was there.

Slocum drew a breath and held on to it while shifting to face Ed's horse.

Vaccaro backed away, a venomous look spreading across his face. His eyes shifted between Ed's saddlebags and Slocum, who stood sideways so his back was partly to him.

Ed saw Vaccaro bring his gun up and meant to shout a warning to Slocum. His fingers even tightened around the .44's handle, but by the time he'd drawn the weapon, Slocum had already pivoted and snatched a Colt from his own holster. Two guns barked in quick succession. After that, Ed hunkered down and fired a shot from his .44.

For a moment, Ed thought he'd caught a piece of lead in the gut. Vaccaro, on the other hand, fared much worse.

The robber stood his ground, smoking gun in hand. His barrel was angled toward the ground and a stunned expression was etched onto his face. He blinked once, coughed up some blood, and dropped to his knees. More blood flowed from a hole in his chest as he spat out part of a grunted obscenity and then flopped onto his side.

Slocum stood his ground, holding his pistol at hip level. A long mound of dirt had been upturned near his feet, presumably by the bullet that had come from Vaccaro's pistol. He stalked forward, nudged the robber with his boot, and then stooped down to take the gun from Vaccaro's hand. Turning to face Ed, he asked, "You hit?"

"I . . . I'm not . . ." Ed stammered. Still feeling a pinching pain in his gut, Ed hesitated before moving. Finally, he started to sit upright. The pain jabbed at his innards, fading slightly as he straightened. "I don't think so," he finally said. "Probably just a nervous stomach."

Slocum watched as Ed prodded his midsection. "I don't see any blood," he said. "You should be fine." After tucking one pistol into his holster and the other under his belt, he turned to walk away.

"Wait a second!" Ed shouted. "Don't just leave."

"I'm going to fetch someone to clean up this mess."

"You mean like a lawman?"

"Either that or an undertaker," Slocum replied. "Whichever's first to answer the call, I suppose."

"Then what?"

"Then I'm having a drink."

Ed flicked his reins, but his horse wouldn't move. The animal was trembling on account of the shots that had been fired. Rather than risk the horse bolting while he was still in the saddle, Ed climbed down and led it by the reins as he rushed to catch up with the other man. "Hold up," he said while placing a hand on Slocum's shoulder.

Slocum stopped and spun around, fixing Ed with a glare that made him pull his hand back real quick.

"I don't mean to be rude," Ed explained. "I'd like to thank you for helping me back there. My name's Ed Warren."

Now that Ed's hand had been lowered and extended toward him, the other man nodded and shook it. "John Slocum."

"So . . . you know that man?" Ed asked while risking half a glance back at the spot where Vaccaro lay. "Or . . . *knew* him?"

"He's just some piece of trash that blew in from Saint Louis. Been talking tough and stealing from drunks or anyone else who he thinks won't stand up to him. I don't like them kind, so I told him to get the hell out of this town."

"I don't much like them kind either. Men like that one back there killed some good folks that were riding with me. Burned one of our wagons and made off with a lot of our belongings."

"You think they're friends of his?" Slocum asked, staring down at Vaccaro as if the dead man might stand up and challenge him one last time.

Ed looked down at Vaccaro, over at Slocum, back to Vaccaro, and then back to Slocum before finally sputtering, "N-No, I mean they were men like him. As in similar. Bad men. Killers."

Slocum chuckled once and turned his back on the carcass as if the former robber was no more than a pile of trash. "Vaccaro wished he was a bad man. I've seen plenty that were a whole lot worse. You want to have a drink with me? Looks like you could use one."

2

Ed's hands were trembling. "I could definitely use a drink. But . . . shouldn't we wait here for the law or whoever will clean this up?"

"I reckon someone will find us before we get to the River Wheel."

Now that they were walking down the street, Ed could see the River Wheel Saloon up past the next corner. He'd only been to Saint Joseph twice before, which wasn't enough for him to be familiar with the place. All he knew was the way out of town, but something kept him from taking that very attractive prospect just yet. "I ought to buy you that drink."

"Yes," Slocum replied with a wry smirk, "you should."

They were halfway to the corner when Ed asked, "So you were out looking for that Vaccaro fella?"

"Nope."

"Then you knew there could be trouble?"

"Not as such."

Ed kept staring at Slocum, which did nothing to elicit a response. "So what were you doing at that spot at that particular time?"

"I was headed to the general store for some coffee," Slocum said. "Tomorrow I'm riding out. Speaking of which . . ."

"Yes?" Ed chirped as he watched a man walk straight for them with purpose in his strides.

"I still need coffee."

"Mr. Slocum," the purposeful man said. He wore a dusty Stetson and a rumpled yellow shirt beneath a wool-lined jacket. His wide face bore a smile that was as short on humor as it was on patience. "I heard shots. Am I wrong in thinking you were in the vicinity when they were fired?"

Slocum stopped and hooked his thumbs over his gun belt. "I was there, Sheriff. Vaccaro meant to kill me."

"What happened?"

"I killed him first."

The man in the Stetson turned to face Ed. He placed his hands upon his hips so as to display the star pinned to his shirt pocket as well as the gun strapped around his waist. "And who might you be?"

"Ed Warren, sir. I came by to visit a friend of mine from way back."

"You know Mr. Slocum here?"

"Only just got introduced," Ed said while lifting his chin. "He saved my life."

"Yeah, well, don't let that color your expectations," the sheriff said. "Most folks who spend too much time around him just get shot."

Slocum took that barb in good humor. "I'm sure you don't mind the occasional shot being fired around here," he said. "Especially since it means someone else is doing your job for you."

The big lawman nodded. "Speaking of my job, I've got some business to tend to right now. I believe you owe me some money."

That brought an end to Slocum's good humor. "What for?"

"The disturbance just now. Seems there's a dead body that wasn't there before."

"I told you Vaccaro meant to kill me," Slocum said.

"And I believe you, which is why I'm not hauling you away right now. Instead, I'm fining you for disturbance of the peace and for taking the law into your own hands. Also, after your last confrontation with Mr. Vaccaro, I recall asking you to hand in your weapon and not fire another one within town limits."

"How much is the fine?"

After milking the next few moments by scratching his chin thoughtfully, the lawman told him, "Two hundred sounds about right."

"I don't have that much."

"Then perhaps there's still a cage in your future," the sheriff said, punctuating his statement with a sharp jab of his finger against Slocum's chest.

Slocum stared directly into the sheriff's eyes. His body tensed in a way that made the air crackle like a storm that was less than a minute away from spilling rain onto the town. Ed could feel more violence approaching and didn't have the first idea of what to do about it. Before he was forced to run or pick sides, Slocum defused the situation by reaching into his pocket and pulling out a slim wad of bills. "This is all I have," he said.

The sheriff snatched the money away from him as if he was expecting repercussions. All he got was a look from Slocum that could have peeled the paint off the side of a barn. "I only count seventy-five dollars here."

"Take it," Slocum growled.

"You know I will." Good to his word, the lawman pocketed the money and stepped up so he was close enough to butt heads with Slocum. He leaned in and stopped just shy of knocking his hat against the other man's forehead. "Next time there's a problem in town, you find me. And the next time you decide to leave another body on one of my streets, you should bring enough to pay the piper. Hand over that gun next time you pass my office."

"You're the piper, huh?" Slocum chuckled. "I suppose you spout more than enough wind to fit that bill."

The sheriff continued to nod as he walked away. The moment he saw he was being watched by a group of locals, he raised both hands and strolled toward the building behind which Vaccaro's body was lying. "Everyone just take it easy! I'm sorting this mess out right now. Go about your business, folks!"

Slocum furrowed his brow and let out a breath that appeared as steam curling from between his lips. "Think I'll need two drinks."

"They're both on me, friend," Ed was quick to say.

"They'd better be. What money I got stashed in my boots is hardly enough to see me through a day or two. If that pig found out I had that much, he'd scrounge for it himself."

"I thought he would take your gun," Ed said.

"Nah. Then he wouldn't have an excuse to fine me again later."

When the two of them got to the River Wheel Saloon, Ed tied his horse to a post outside and followed Slocum into a room that was somehow warm and inviting despite the fact that it stank of stale cigar smoke and spilled beer. Slocum approached the bar, slapped his hand against it, and asked for a bottle of whiskey with a pair of glasses. Once Ed came up beside him, Slocum pushed one of the glasses over to him and said, "I don't expect you to buy the whole bottle. Just chip in for your share."

"I will buy the bottle," Ed said loudly enough for the barkeep to hear. "I'll need it to keep me warm for the ride back to Nebraska."

"Cold time of year for that trip," Slocum mused. "Much easier during the spring."

"We headed out months ago, but were delayed by a bad bit of luck involving those robbers I mentioned earlier."

Slocum tipped his glass back and allowed the firewater

to run its course through his body. "That's right. You did mention it."

"We tried to get going sooner, since it became clear that the longer we waited, the poorer we'd become."

"That's usually how it works."

"Yes sir, it is," Ed sighed. He took his drink and winced slightly at the burn that started at the back of his throat and became a more bearable heat as it trickled down. "Sounds like you've had a recent spot of trouble yourself, Mr. Slocum."

"Might as well call me John. And yeah. There was some trouble. Nothing that a lawman who works to earn his pay couldn't fix." Slocum was sure to say that last part loudly enough for his words to carry throughout the saloon. Most of the folks in there either raised their glasses or had better things to do than grouse about the local civil servants. Lowering his voice to a more sociable level, Slocum said, "There was a dispute over a gambling debt."

"What . . . uh . . . what kind of dispute?"

"Some asshole swore two pair beat three of a kind and he thought he could prove it with a knife."

"What did you do?"

"Waited until I was sure he meant business and shot him. Last time he ever gets confused about the pecking order in poker hands. He was a loud son of a bitch anyway. Would've jumped me soon as I left that table with my winnings. Vaccaro and a few others tried that very thing and I shot most of them, too. Messy affair, but not my fault. That sheriff warned me to get out of town. Called me a troublemaker. Can you believe that?"

"Yes," Ed replied. "I can believe it."

Slocum looked over at him with newfound respect. He then slapped him on the back and laughed wholeheartedly. "You got a good head on your shoulders, Ed. I like that."

"Great! Then maybe you wouldn't mind riding with me and my wagons out to Colorado?"

Frozen with a glass to his lips, Slocum eased it back down to the bar and reached for the bottle. "Why would I want to do that? Hell, for that matter, why would *you* want me to do that?"

"Because we could use a man to ride with us for protection. We're headed through Indian territory."

"You'd be dealing with the Pawnee and Cheyenne, most likely. Stick to the trail, mind your manners, and you'll most likely be all right. Or are you more worried about another robber gang looking to finish the job the first one started?"

"They're all concerns." Pushing away the glass containing the last bit of his whiskey, Ed said, "We're five wagons and nine good people. Ten if you count me. Three are children, three are women, and one is an old man who does the cooking. Apart from me, only one of us is any good with a rifle. We've already been hit hard once, John. Can't afford to be hit again."

"Then maybe you should consider turning around and going back to where you come from."

"We struck out from Illinois hailing from as far east as Boston. We've all come too far to just head back now."

"Then have your wagons sit tight where they are. There are plenty of folks who make camp for a season or two while scraping together some money to push on. I'd say that's your best prospect. Especially," Slocum added, "since it seems this journey of yours is something close to cursed as it is."

"Are you trying to discourage me?" Ed asked.

"Yeah. I am. And if you think about the trials and losses you've already told me about, you'd probably agree with my reasoning."

Ed shook his head solemnly. "All them good people I told you about threw in with me for a reason. I swore to get them to Colorado and that's what I intend to do."

"I'm sure they'd rather have you make some changes to that plan before more of them were killed."

That struck a nerve within Ed. It was as plain to see as the twitch on his face and the tension in his hand as he nearly drove his fingers through the bar. Finally, he picked up his glass so he could finish the last sip of whiskey. "If we turn back, all our sacrifice would be for nothing. Also, we'd probably just be going straight into the sights of the same men that burned our wagons in the first place."

"Didn't the law round them up?"

"Mostly. The ones that got away surely reached out to some friends of their own. If murderous animals like that truly have friends."

Slocum let out a slow breath and gazed straight across at a row of dusty bottles on the shelf behind the bar. "Men like that always got friends," he said. "Animals tend to run in packs."

"Even if we were heading back, we'd still need someone to watch out for us. Seeing as how we all sold everything we owned for a better chance in the Rockies, turning back just doesn't make much sense."

"The Rockies, huh? Making your way through the mountains can be a whole lot rougher than crossing a prairie."

"I know that," Ed snapped. "I ain't stupid. None of us are. We're a group of investors who pitched in to buy the rights to a whole mess of mining claims that were put up for sale through a broker friend of mine. He's the same fellow I know here in town. And since I cashed in what little credit and favors I had with him, me and everyone else in that wagon train are in this up to our ears. There's no road back, and even if there was, we wouldn't take it."

Slocum leaned an elbow against the bar. "Sounds to me like you and the rest of your bunch are in up to this higher than your ears. Maybe higher than you can manage."

"Maybe so," Ed admitted. "That's why I'm asking for your help. We can pay you."

"I thought you were a group of impoverished pioneers. How do you intend on paying me?"

"We've still got funds for the rest of the journey. Before we started looking for another gun arm, we agreed on what we'd pay such a man should he agree to join up with us. I'm sure I don't need to tell you what sort of opportunities there are for any man in a land as rich as Colorado. Or . . . perhaps I do."

"No, I've heard the sales pitch a few times," Slocum replied. "Even been out that way myself a time or two."

Lowering his voice, Ed continued, "Part of your fee would be shares in a few of those mines I mentioned."

"I'm no miner."

"There's already been gold discovered in all of these claims. It's not a lot, which is why they're being sold. The broker who collected the deeds doesn't have the funds or compunction to head out there to work the mines himself, but they're genuine enough."

"And how do you know that? This supposed friend told you so? A man your age should know better than to believe what anyone tells you where distant gold claims are concerned. That's one of the oldest tricks in the book, especially when the ones being duped won't find out they've been had until they're hundreds of miles away with no means to get back."

Those words hit Ed like a punch to the stomach, and he poured another drink to cushion the blow. Before he could lift the glass, it was held down against the bar.

"Answer me something, Ed," Slocum said while keeping the other man from having his drink. "How many people did you say are on this wagon train of yours?"

Without blinking, Ed replied, "Ten including me."

"And where are they now?"

"Headed into Nebraska. We were to take a trail leading from Omaha all the way into Colorado. Long as the man I left in charge follows the plan, he'll start heading southwest just east of Lincoln. Once they do, they're to set up camp and wait for me to catch up to them."

Slocum's eyes bored into Ed like a pair of drills. His hand lifted away, freeing Ed to have his whiskey. "I make it a general rule to never trust someone full of promises of gold and job offers."

"I'm no liar, Mr. Slocum."

"Yeah. I can see as much. Either that, or you're a damn good one. Whichever it is, I don't have much business left to conduct here in town. In fact, as you've already seen, I've got one big fat reason wearing a star on his chest to put this place behind me and not look back."

"Being on the law's bad side is a tough row to hoe," Ed agreed. "Also, it sounds like you're short on funds after that gambling business and those fines that were levied."

"I've been poor plenty of times and will be plenty more times again before it's all said and done. What really matters isn't the money or lack of it. The important thing for me is to keep from letting grass grow beneath my feet."

"Even so," Ed added with a chuckle, "money doesn't hurt."

"No sir, it most certainly does not." Slapping the bar like a judge rapping his gavel, Slocum asked, "So what's my fee without factoring in those mining claims?"

Ed couldn't help looking away when he said, "A hundred and fifty dollars. Maybe a little less depending on how long it takes to get across Nebraska. Of course you won't have to worry about food or shelter along the way. At least, the sort of food and shelter we can provide."

"And with the claims?"

Brightening up considerably, Ed replied, "Some of those mines paid out fairly decently last year and that was before they were being worked properly. With me and some of the others working them, you won't have to wait long before you earn at least—"

"All right. I'm sold."

"You . . . you are?"

Slocum nodded, examined what remained inside the whiskey bottle, and then stuffed the cork back into it. "I won't force you to speculate on how much you'll pull out of some mine. I've been meaning to get back to Leadville anyway, but the train tickets are no longer within my price range. Also, this here town has worn thin with me. When do we leave?"

"Tomorrow morning. Bright and early."

3

Ed woke up before sunrise the next morning, eager to shake the dust of Saint Joseph from his boots. When he didn't find Slocum there to meet him at the spot they'd agreed upon before parting ways the previous night, he wondered if he'd been swindled for something as little as a bottle of whiskey. But Slocum arrived a few minutes later, somewhat worse for the wear.

"Forgot to mention," he said as he rode up on the sloped back of a dark gray mare with light speckles in her coat, "I'm gonna need a new horse. That's part of my fee and I don't want it to come out of the rest of it."

Narrowing his eyes, Ed asked, "Is this some sort of bonus . . . in advance of you doing anything to earn it?"

"You could think of it that way. Or you could consider it a show of good faith. Or . . . you could consider it a favor for the man who saved your life."

"I suppose, when you put it that way, it seems like a fairly decent offer."

"I thought so," Slocum said. "There are some fine horses being sold down the street. Good prices, too."

"You'll have your new horse once we meet up with the wagons," Ed told him. "They're from hearty stock and are plenty strong enough to make it the rest of the way."

"What about the ride into Nebraska? You think I can make it on this bag of bones?"

Ed walked over to Slocum's horse and began circling the animal while examining it from head to toe. Slocum sat impatiently in his saddle, biting his tongue until Ed was through. Finally, with a solid pat on the gray horse's rump, Ed declared, "This gal may be old, but she's got plenty of ride left in her. Enough to make it to where we're going anyway. Once we're there, I'll trade you for one of the horses in my own team."

"No trade," Slocum said. "I'll sell this horse off first chance I get after buckling my saddle over a better one."

"Pitch in twenty-five percent of the sale to the travel fund and you've got a deal."

"Ten percent."

"Fifteen."

Slocum pondered that for all of three seconds before extending his hand. "You got a deal, but only if the horse you're offering is worth it."

Ed shook his hand. "You're coming out ahead in this deal, I promise you."

"You're a hell of a trader," Slocum said with a subtle nod. "Should do well when you get a business of your own."

"I've had businesses of my own, Mr. Slocum. A few of them, in fact. They've all prospered. Once we get to Colorado, I'll be trading up for a business that's even more fruitful."

"I imagine you will. And like I already told you . . . call me John."

The ride from Saint Joseph wasn't a sociable one. Slocum and Ed rode hard from sunup to sundown, resting only when their horses needed it. By the time they made camp, neither man had enough steam to do more than have a sparse meal, stretch out their legs, and fall asleep. Apart from a few passing words, the only sounds to fill their ears were the thunder of hooves upon the cold ground and the rush of wind as they sped northward into Nebraska and then west toward Lincoln.

They met up with the others as the wagons plodded slowly along their appointed trail. As he drew closer to the wagon at the back of the group, Slocum became aware that he was staring down the wrong end of a rifle. His eyes were sharp enough to spot the firearm in the hands of a man on that wagon, but before he could voice his concerns, Ed motioned for him to ease back while he snapped his reins to charge forward.

"It's me, Josiah!" Ed hollered. "Put that rifle away!"

The voice that came back was harsh as gravel scraping against the bottom of a tin pan. "Who's that with ya?"

"This man will be riding with us!"

"You hired a gun?"

"Just put the rifle away!"

Even from a distance, Slocum could read the rifleman's hesitance as he lowered the rifle from his shoulder and eased back down into the driver's seat. After that, all he could see was the back of the wagon swaying to and fro as its wheels clattered over a bumpy stretch of trail. Slocum flicked his reins to coax some more speed from his horse. The poor old gal had started wheezing during the latter portion of the previous day's ride, and he knew she wouldn't be able to go much farther at anything quicker than a brisk walk. Fortunately, the wagons ground to a halt to meet both riders before Slocum's horse spat its last breath.

The man with the rifle stood up after setting his brake to prop one leg upon the edge of the seat and his rifle stock against his hip. He had a body that looked more like a set of bones wrapped in dusty clothes and a face that was covered in coarse stubble. Dark eyes were narrowed into slits from staring for too long down the sights of his Winchester. Easing a battered hat farther up along his head, he said, "Thought we gave up on hiring on a gunman."

"This here is John Slocum," Ed announced. "And he's no gunman."

"If he ain't handy with a gun, then we don't need him."

"Mind your manners and give him a proper welcome. John, this is Josiah Pincher."

Slocum rode forward and shook a hand that felt more like a bird's talon. "Pleased to meet you," he said. "And just put your mind at ease, I can handle a gun just fine."

"But he's not just some gunfighter," Ed was quick to point out. "He's a good man who saved my life in Saint Joseph. He'll do just fine to see to it that we all make it into Colorado."

By now, several other faces were emerging from within some of the wagons or rising up over others like prairie dogs poking their noses up from their mounds. The last wagon was Josiah's and it looked to be stuffed full of blankets and large items like bureaus and tables. The next wagon in line rattled noisily even after it had come to a stop, thanks to the pots and pans hanging from a rack just inside the wooden frame. More rattling came from inside that wagon as other cooking implements were knocked against cups, plates, or any number of things put to use by the round-faced man who announced himself to be Franco, the cook. He sported an ample gut on a lanky frame as well as a beard that joined one sideburn to another like the strap of a non-existent helmet.

More introductions came swiftly from there. The wagon in the middle of the group was occupied by a tall woman named Theresa Wilcox. She had black hair that fell in a wave of tight curls well past her shoulders. Her skin was smooth, pale, and as beautiful as her hesitant smile. She displayed no hesitation whatsoever when it came to wrangling the young boy who attempted to jump down from the wagon to get a closer look at Slocum. He was a skinny wisp of a lad with tousled brown hair and a set of wire-framed spectacles that made his eyes look even wider as he stared at the new arrival. "This is my son, James," Theresa said.

The boy continued his attempts to climb down from the wagon, but was held in place by the back of his shirt like a puppy being restrained by the scruff of its neck. "Can I see your pistol?" he asked. "Is that a Colt? What caliber is that? Have you killed anyone? I want to kill someone someday!"

"James!" Theresa scolded. "None of that talk!"

Finally, the boy stopped trying to get away from his mother and instead nestled against her. "I meant I'd kill bad men, Momma."

Theresa patted her son's head and shook hers at Slocum by way of an exasperated apology.

The next wagon was teeming with even more activity. Two children crawled inside, tugging at the tarp so they could alternate between peeking out through the back and hiding when Slocum's eyes came anywhere close to finding them. One was a girl with straw-colored hair and pale skin. Slocum couldn't see much more than that because she was doing most of the hiding. A young boy with thick, dark, curly hair and large eyes struggled to open the back of the wagon a little more, but was held back by the girl. A woman with a long face leaned over from the driver's seat to get a look at Slocum while a large man climbed down to approach him directly.

"If Ed speaks for you, that's good enough for me," said the man, who was a few inches shorter than Slocum but several inches wider. His hat hung around his neck as if it was unsuited for the task of covering his large head, which, in turn, was covered by a thick mat of hair arranged in unruly curls that had most definitely been passed on to the boy in the wagon. "I'm Tom McCauley. That's my wife, Vera."

The woman lifted herself up a bit so she could wave

tentatively at Slocum. She had a cautious demeanor that made her look too weak to lift her hand more than a few inches over her head.

"Those two are my children," Tom continued. "Elsie and Michael."

"Hello," both children said in almost perfect unison.

"Howdy," Slocum replied.

By this time, Ed had already ridden up to the wagon at the front of the line. He swung down from his horse and displayed more spring in his step than he'd shown in the last several days when he raced around to catch the woman who practically jumped down to land in his arms. After the couple had exchanged a few words only they could hear, Ed escorted her over to Slocum. "This is my wife," he said. "May."

May had a light complexion that seemed even fairer due to the golden hair that was kept in place by a bonnet showing all the wear and tear one might expect while riding at the front of a wagon train through the harsh prairie winds. There was a strength about her that made it plain to see she didn't need to be escorted and protected as much as Ed insisted on doing for her, but allowed him to perform those services because she knew he liked doing so. "You're welcome to ride with us, Mr. Slocum," she said. "But it looks like your horse might not be up to the task."

"You made some progress in the last day or so," Ed said. "More than I was expecting. I thought we would catch up to you twenty miles back."

"Just because you dawdled about looking to hire on a gunman when we agreed we didn't need one after all," Josiah grunted, "that don't mean we should sit around waiting for you to grace us with your presence again. For all we knew, you'd fallen from your saddle and broken yer neck."

James gasped at that, but Theresa was there to rub his back and assure him that nobody was going to break their neck.

"No need to frighten the children with that kind of talk,"

May scolded. "Ed was only a day late, but I'm sure there was a good reason for it."

"The ride to Saint Joseph was a bit longer than I recalled," Ed explained. "Also, there was some trouble while I was there." Before either of the anxious little boys could press him for details, Ed quickly added, "But it wasn't anything that I couldn't handle, especially with the help of my new friend here."

Feeling all eyes fixing upon him, Slocum busied himself by climbing down from the saddle and examining his horse.

"And to address what was said before," Ed continued, "he is no gunman. John is capable enough to lend us the assistance we need and he's also got some business to tend to in Colorado. Fortune smiled by bringing us together like it did, so I made him the offer to ride with us and he accepted. I know we'd given up on trying to hire on someone for protection, but when fortune smiles, it ain't wise to ignore it."

Noticing the sour expression on Josiah's face, Slocum said, "As far as my gun arm goes, it's strong enough to do the job you folks need done. I'm also no stranger to scouting, riding, or anything else you people could need. I guarantee you I'll earn my fee."

"How much is that fee?" Josiah asked.

"That's business to be discussed later," Ed told him.

"Better not be the same we talked about earlier," the skinny rifleman said. "That was only if we all got to approve him."

"Business for later, I said."

Josiah sighed and locked eyes with Slocum. For a moment it looked like he might fire a shot at him from the rifle in his hands. Instead, he grunted under his breath and placed the Winchester where he could get to it at a moment's notice.

"Yes sir," Slocum said under his breath. "It's a long way to Colorado."

4

The wagon train rumbled across the prairies of Nebraska with mountainous regions in their sights. The winds were harsh and sprouted icy claws as the sun went down, giving everyone a taste of what was surely to be a horrific winter. Slocum was given another gray horse to take the place of the one he'd ridden from Missouri, but this one was a gelding with a thick coat that was the color of dense fog at early evening. It was a spirited animal that seemed plenty happy to be relieved from its duty at the front of Ed's wagon where it could run away from the other teams beneath a rider that was equally glad to strike out on his own.

Slocum's primary duty was to ensure the safety of the wagons and the people within them. In the absence of any immediate dangers, he acted as scout and rode ahead to get a look at the trail as well as the terrain they were about to cross. In the first day he rode with them, Ed and May were some of the only ones to truly make him feel welcome. The children gave him anxious little grins, and the rest made do with uncomfortable small talk. For the most part, that was all just fine with Slocum.

The next day was a little easier. Part of that was because it couldn't have started on a better foot thanks to the biscuits and gravy cooked up by Franco. As the sun crested the horizon, Franco emerged from his wagon and bustled about the fire like a man possessed. It was an amusing sight considering the fact that he was a slender man apart from a bulbous belly that protruded from his midsection like a pregnant woman's bulge. He cooked the biscuits and slathered them in gravy that was thick with large chunks of ham and sausage.

"There's no way this could taste as good as it smells," Slocum said as he approached the front of the line for his portion.

Franco stopped with gravy dripping from his ladle onto the biscuits he'd piled onto the plate in his hand. "Is that a joke?"

"Not at all."

"You're insulting my food?"

"No, I'm just saying it smells too good to be true." Weathering the cook's angry glare, Slocum dipped his spoon into the gravy once he was handed his plate. The spoon went into his mouth and was barely out again before he proclaimed, "Turns out this is a rare case indeed. This is actually better than it smells and I would have paid a pretty penny just to smell something like this in damn near any restaurant."

"Please, Mr. Slocum," Vera McCauley said. "Watch your language."

It seemed Vera was the only one to take offense. The children in the vicinity still gazed upon Slocum as if he were a carnival exhibit, and Franco was doing a poor job of containing the pride that swelled his chest to tax the already strained seams of his shirt. That day was a long one, since it involved crossing a stream that had swollen enough to obscure enough half-buried logs and deep trenches to potentially send several of the wagons to the bottom. After hours spent testing dozens of different potential crossings, Slocum, Ed, Tom, and Josiah found a path that delivered all the wagons safely to the other side.

When Franco prepared a simple lunch of bacon sandwiches and beans, Slocum and the other men were still soaked to the bone. That chill had worked all the way down to the core of Slocum's body when supper was served, but he was still able to shake it off while enjoying a thick beefy stew. He fell asleep near the fire while James Wilcox told him everything he'd learned in his short life about Indian tribes and the bloody battles fought by the Sioux.

Sharing meals with James Wilcox and his mother quickly became a habit for Slocum. Considering how lively the boy's stories were and how focused he was on anything Slocum said in return, it wasn't much of a chore. Once Theresa warmed up to him enough for her to sit beside Slocum and laugh at some of his bad jokes, it became a downright pleasure. Everyone in the wagon train had accepted Slocum by then, but Theresa showed him more than just accommodating politeness. Every night, she sat a little closer to him, smiled a bit longer when he looked in her direction, and finally lingered a bit longer whenever he found a way to brush against her warm body or touch the thick curls of her hair.

They'd enjoyed each other's company from the first moment they had a chance to talk without the rest of the wagon train watching them. They'd gotten closer on the third night after he'd signed on with them. Slocum had been riding alongside the wagons, watching the horizon, while Ed took his turn scouting ahead. It hadn't taken long for Slocum to get beside Theresa's wagon and match its pace.

They'd started off joking about a few things and then he asked about how she'd wound up riding across the country with everything she owned crammed into the back of a wagon. Theresa's husband hadn't been good for much of anything apart from giving her James. He was a drunkard with a mean streak and a coward who could only unleash that streak upon a woman and small child. She'd left him and wouldn't accept charity, but prospects were slim. Slim, that is, until she got an opportunity to throw in with a small group of prospectors who were in need of backers as well as able bodies to help work a claim. Theresa had strong hands and a quick enough tongue to convince Ed that she'd be an invaluable addition to the group. She wanted a fresh start for herself and her son and had the means to head out on Ed's schedule. Making the trip with them marked the end of her savings and was an all-or-nothing proposition for her. That, in itself, made her just like everyone else driving those wagons into Colorado.

Slocum's story didn't have as many pieces as hers. He told her how he'd wound up in Saint Joseph, which was simply a stop on his way from Saint Louis. He'd gone to Missouri in the first place to visit an old friend. When that friend begged to borrow money to get back on his feet after yet another failed business venture, Slocum handed over what money he had as a way to cut ties with the so-called friend with a clear conscience. He'd barely had enough to buy a run-down horse and had been working his way across the state to check in with another acquaintance who owed him money. That acquaintance was nowhere to be found, leaving Slocum in the lurch. He took a few jobs, wound up in Saint Joseph, and met up with Ed.

He and Theresa spent a good portion of that day joking about the uselessness of old acquaintances until it was time to make camp for the night. They'd joked some more and took a walk in the moonlight after everyone else was asleep in their bedrolls. He'd kissed her the first time then and they'd shared several more during the following nights.

While taller than most women, she didn't stoop or try to hide it in any way. She carried herself with pride and a strength that came from fending for herself and her young one for a good, long time. Her eyes were smoky and inviting, and she spoke to him in a rich voice that was easy to turn toward laughter. During the evening after Slocum's first week on the trail with them, he found himself with his back to the fire long after the children had been put to bed. He stared out toward the western horizon, studying the stars, which seemed to sparkle even brighter since the darkness had grown colder.

"Aren't you coming to bed?" Theresa asked while sidling up to stand beside him.

Slocum stood with a large boulder between him and the wagons. The rock wasn't tall enough to hide him completely from the others, but was enough to give a small amount of privacy. His intention had been just to have something solid to lean against for a while, but he was now grateful for the makeshift barrier. "Did someone dig out a bed for me to use?" he asked.

She laughed and wrapped her arms around herself to hold her woolen shawl in place. "I guess that just sounded better than me asking if you plan on coming back so you can sleep on the ground wrapped up in a bunch of dirty blankets. After all, a question like that might make you want to throw your saddle on your horse and ride in the opposite direction while our backs were turned."

"Don't worry. You folks are stuck with me for a while."

"Not stuck," she said softly. "Not hardly."

"What brings you out here so far from the fire?"

"You do."

Slocum turned to get a look at her. In the last several days, he'd been noticing her more and more. Her dark hair and pretty face had struck him from the moment they'd been introduced, but it wasn't long before he found his thoughts lingering on the shapely curves of her body and the long legs he imagined were beneath the skirts she always wore. Her hands were strong and her skin was smooth, taking his thoughts in other directions on cold nights such as this. Doing his best to keep his face from betraying those thoughts, even in the shadows, he said, "I'm on watch tonight."

"Does there really seem to be a danger of being robbed again? I would think it'd be like lightning," she said with an uneasy laugh. "Get struck once and the odds are pretty slim of getting struck again."

"There's a lot of men who might see these wagons as an easy target. More of them than lightning strikes, I'd wager. Then there's animals that could come after our food or the horses. There's also—"

She stopped him with a hand placed on his arm. "I understand. Any more of your explanation and you might make me too nervous to sleep."

"Sorry about that. Guess it's my nature to think about all the angles, no matter how grim some of them might be."

"That's how a man survives on his own in this world." She moved in closer and took a seat beside him. When she leaned against him, it seemed like the most natural thing in the world. "How long have you been on your own?"

After a short bit of contemplation, Slocum told her, "Long enough that it doesn't seem to matter anymore."

She pressed herself against him, leaned over, and whispered, "It matters."

Slocum turned toward her and placed the edge of one finger beneath her chin. That way, he could lift her face just enough to kiss her on the lips. It was a long, lingering kiss that had the added spice of being stolen while no one was looking. Slocum felt a rush through his entire body when he wrapped her in his arms and laid her down on the blanket he'd been using to cushion himself from the cold, hard ground.

Theresa seemed reluctant at first, but the quick glances toward the wagons let Slocum know she was more worried about being discovered than what was actually happening. "Don't worry," he whispered. "As long as we're quiet, we can hear anything bigger than a field mouse that comes toward us."

"That's the problem," she said. "I don't know if I can be quiet with you."

Now, there was no mistaking that she wanted him just as much as he wanted her. If there was any shred of doubt in his mind, it was erased when she positioned herself beneath him and started tugging at his belt to loosen it. First, the gun belt came off and was placed within easy reach. Next, she worked on his jeans while Slocum eased his hands up under her skirts. After navigating through layers of cloth and slips, he found the cotton undergarments separating him from where he wanted to be. Slocum tried pulling them off her carefully at first, but the urgency that had been building inside both of them boiled over until he ripped her undergarments off. The only other sound apart from the tearing fabric was the excited groan issuing from the back of Theresa's throat.

She froze in place, leaning her head back to once again look toward the wagons. She couldn't see them because of the rock at their backs, but she listened intently for any hint of movement approaching their spot. Slocum listened as well, and when he heard nothing but the wind, he slid his hand between her legs until his fingers found their way to the soft thatch of hair between her thighs.

Theresa arched her back and tightened her grip on his arms as Slocum started rubbing her pussy. Her eyes clenched shut and she opened her legs so he could reach in farther and vigorously stroke her. Before long, her entire body began to tremble and she fought the impulse to cry out. When her eyes snapped open again, she looked as if she was on a mission to tear his clothes off as quickly as humanly possible.

Having already started on his jeans, she pulled them open the rest of the way and tugged them down. She barely finished that job before turning her attention to his shirt. Slocum had shifted his focus as well, using both hands to loosen the ties at the front of her dress so he could get his hands upon her warm, bare breasts. And then, like a harsh reminder of where they were, a cold wind tore in from the north to stop them both in their tracks.

"Maybe . . . this isn't such a good idea," Theresa reluctantly said.

Slocum's only response was to take the blanket they'd been using as a mat, unfold it, and drape it over them as protection from the cold. Once the wind was no longer slicing into them and they each had the other's body for warmth, their hands began probing once more and Theresa lay on her back to look up at Slocum as well as the stars above.

Her dress was a rumpled mess around her, more like another blanket than anything she could actually wear. Without all the ties or fasteners in place, she wriggled most of the way out of it with ease. Slocum kicked his boots off and slid out of his jeans. His penis was rigid and Theresa wasted no time in reaching down to feel it for herself. Once her hand was wrapped around him, she started stroking. Her eyes locked on to his to watch his face register every bit of pleasure she was giving him. He reached down to her pussy once more, finding it even wetter than before. Settling on top of her, Slocum felt her legs open wide to accept him. Theresa maintained her grip on his shaft, guiding him toward her moist opening.

Slocum closed his eyes, savoring the moment when the tip of his cock brushed against the lips of her pussy. When he entered her, the cold around them was no longer an issue. He drove all the way inside and stayed there. Theresa's arms wrapped around him, holding him in place.

"God, I've wanted this," she whispered. "Feels . . . so good."

There was a smile on her face. It was a faraway expression as she craned her head back and moved her hands up and down along Slocum's back. When he pumped into her, she let out a grunt, which was quickly stifled before it turned into anything louder. As Slocum drove into her again and again, he realized that he, too, needed to watch how much noise he made. While he was never one to care much for what others thought of him, he didn't want to make things uncomfortable for Theresa among the people in the wagon train, who'd become like a close-knit family. Those thoughts were nothing but a fleeting thing rushing through his mind, however, since Slocum had plenty more to think about.

He thought about how good it felt to bury his cock into Theresa's warm, wet pussy.

He thought about the way her body tensed beneath him or the way she bucked her hips in time to his thrusts after wrapping her legs around him.

He thought about the way she clawed at his back through his shirt and how wild she must be if she could truly let go and give in to every little desire that crossed her mind.

When he slowed down for a while and then pounded into her even harder, he could feel her tighten around him while her entire body quivered. She bit down on her lower lip and pressed her face against Slocum's shoulder so her moans were muffled as she climaxed.

Then, she was squirming as if she was trying to get out from beneath the weight of his body.

"What are you doing?" he asked.

"You made me feel so good," she replied. "I want you to feel good, too."

"Just stay where you are," he told her. "I'm about to feel plenty good."

She wore a little smirk as she crawled out from under him and pushed him onto his back. From there, she crawled on top of him and kissed his mouth, neck, and chest. Slocum could feel the wet lips between her legs brushing against his rigid pole as she kissed him. And then, when she moved beneath the blanket to put her head between his legs, he was truly driven to the brink.

Theresa's mouth was soft as it wrapped around the tip of his penis. Her tongue was warm against his cock and she took every inch of it inside as she eased her head all the way down. Slocum enjoyed her attentions, but still craved to be inside her so he could finish the job he'd started. That craving was forgotten as soon as Theresa's tongue began slipping up and down along his member while her head bobbed up and down.

Slocum had had other women use their mouth on him, but Theresa's was magic. She sped up or slowed down as if she knew exactly how he wanted her to move. Just when he thought she'd taken him to the height of pleasure, she started sucking on him while her tongue teased the underside of his pole.

"Jesus," Slocum grunted. Now he was the one who had to contain himself before drawing too much attention. But he wasn't worried about that any longer. Foremost on his mind was placing his hands on either side of her head and enjoying the rest of what she was giving him.

Theresa's hands moved over his hips and up along his chest. Lowering her head, she took Slocum's penis into her mouth all the way down to its base. Then, as she slowly lifted her head, she sucked him and fluttered her tongue against his sensitive flesh.

He couldn't take it any longer. Slocum's body tensed and the bottoms of his feet pressed against the ground as his pleasure raced toward its conclusion. When he climaxed, he grit his teeth and drew a deep breath while exploding into her mouth. She drank him down until she'd had every drop. When she eased away from him, Slocum wouldn't have been able to get to his feet if a pack of wolves had been charging toward him.

"My goodness," she said while licking the corner of her mouth. "You're trembling."

"Must be the cold," he said weakly.

She climbed to her feet, straightened her dress so it fell more or less where it should, and then fastened enough of the clasps and ties to keep it in place. "Yes," she chuckled. "I'm sure it's just the cold."

Slocum watched her circle around the rock and lean over to take a look at the wagons. The coast must have been clear because she gave him an offhanded wave before walking back to the main campsite. After she was gone, he pulled his clothes back on and bundled the blanket so it could be used as a backrest again.

It was a cold night and the air felt as if it would only get colder with each day that passed. For the moment, however, Slocum didn't feel the slightest chill.

5

The next morning, Theresa tried to act as if nothing had happened. She and James awoke around the same time as the others, came to the cook fire, and helped make preparations for the day while Franco put breakfast together. The morning meal consisted of griddle cakes and bacon with syrup that the cook insisted was imported all the way from Canada. Slocum wasn't an expert on maple syrup, but he knew good griddle cakes when he tasted them and he tasted plenty of them before saddling his horse and heading out.

Scouting was a relaxing affair, simply because there wasn't much to see apart from bare trees and flat terrain that was beginning to show signs of hills and steeper slopes. It wouldn't be long before they crossed into Colorado and not long after that before they caught their first glimpse of the Rockies.

In the days since he'd acquired his new horse, Slocum could tell the animal was growing accustomed to him. Subtle motions of the reins and the occasional touch of his feet against the horse's sides were all that he needed to guide it. Finding his way back to the wagon train was done at an

Before Slocum could wonder how someone could lose count of men who had taken a run at them while in the open, he felt a dizziness that sent a shiver through his eyeballs. The harder he tried to focus, the more difficult that simple task became. The leaves attached to the closest attacker fluttered and twisted in a breeze that wasn't there. One second, the figure seemed to be hunching down and leaning to the left, and the next, it was swaying to the right.

Another figure walked forward, carrying a staff with what looked to be a small animal's head on top of it. The dirty, blurry figures formed a crude circle around this one and became still when the gruesome staff was lifted high.

"Who are you?" Slocum wheezed. Drawing the breath to speak had been much more painful than he'd anticipated. When he didn't get a response, he shouted, "Why did you attack us?"

"You, white men," the one with the staff said, "are trespassers."

"This is open territory," Slocum said.

"*No!* This ground is sacred. You insult it with the imprint of your wicked bodies. You scar it with the wheels of your wagons."

Ed stepped around Slocum's horse, but he wasn't the only one to enter Slocum's field of vision. A few other shapes came into sight and converged on the figure covered in dirt and leaves. While they were also caked in similar grime, more of their bodies could be seen. They were lean men with bare, dark-skinned chests. Rather than just being covered in dirt, they wore it more like decoration.

"We're on our way into Colorado," Ed insisted. "We're not going to harm anyone and never had any intention of settling anywhere near here."

"That is what all white men say. You will turn your wagons around and leave. *Leave*," the earthen figure said, "or *die.*"

And then, like hazy mirages, the figures crouched down and disappeared.

"Keep flapping your gums the way you've been doing and I'll show you what this boy can—"

A sound rolled in from the south that was part wailing cry and part howl. Slocum turned toward the direction from which it had come, only to find the same bunch of hills rising gradually to a low rise less than half a mile from the trail. He'd circled around behind those hills less than an hour ago and couldn't see anything on them now apart from stalks of grass and patches of weeds that were too stubborn to die in the mounting chill.

"What the hell was that?" Slocum asked.

Josiah propped one foot upon the boards in front of him. "How should I know? I'm just driving this here wagon. The man that should know is the one paid to do the scouting."

Before Josiah had even gotten the last of his words out, Slocum's horse was kicking up dust as he urged it to race toward those hills. Behind him, Ed shouted, "You need some help, John?"

Slocum knew better than to waste any time with a reply so he just kept riding.

Ed watched him for a few more seconds before motioning for the wagons to come to a halt. After setting his brake, he climbed down from the wagon and untied one of the horses secured to a hitch on the side of the wagon. "Anyone else tries to follow me," he said to his wife, "tell them to stay put."

"Why?" May said, suddenly worried as she watched her husband climb into the other horse's saddle. "What if both of you need help?"

"And what if something comes at these wagons while both of us are out there? This is why we hired John to come with us. Josiah is here. He and Tom can keep watch. Sending any more than two of us away just to chase a peculiar noise could be too costly."

"That noise was more than peculiar," May said as a chill rolled through her that had nothing to do with the wind.

SLOCUM AND THE SPIRIT BEAR   39

"I know, darlin'. Just stay put and hand me that rifle."

She reached for the Spencer rifle tucked beneath the driver's seat and handed it down to him. When he took the weapon from her, Ed was sure to brush his fingers along his wife's hand for one last bit of her warmth before riding away. Her eyes shifted toward Josiah, who'd settled into his seat with his foot propped up as if it were just another lazy afternoon.

"Miss May!" Little Michael McCauley shouted from the wagon directly behind her. "Did that noise come from a monster?"

"No such things as monsters," she replied.

"Should I ride out with Ed?" Tom McCauley asked.

May stood up and turned around so she could be heard by the rest of the wagons. Her voice was stern and full of authority when she said, "Everyone sit tight and wait here. Ed and John are going to check on whatever that was. Tom, you're to stay here with us."

Tom gripped his rifle and stayed put to guard the women and children. Since she didn't know what the two men were checking on in the first place, May was relieved that nobody asked any more questions.

Slocum pulled back on the reins just enough to slow his horse from a full gallop to a quick trot. Although the animal's hooves still crunched upon the gritty earth, there was a lot less noise than when the wind had been rushing past his face and the ground had been trampled beneath him. When Ed drew closer, Slocum signaled for the other man to slow his horse as well.

"What cried out like that?" Ed asked as he came up alongside Slocum.

"Don't know yet, but I think I saw some movement over by those trees."

Ed squinted in that direction. "Something was definitely moving over yonder. Some branches were set to swaying and . . ." Pausing when he got another quick wave from

Slocum, he finished his thought in a terse whisper. "And something's creeping on the ground."

"Yeah," Slocum replied. "I see that, too."

Set just over the top rise of the hills, the trees stood huddled in a small, tight group like a family relying on each other for warmth. Slocum wasn't about to count them all, but he knew from riding past them earlier that there were more of them leading down the backside of the hills than he could see from here. Even so, he guessed there weren't many more than a dozen or so standing trunks in all. The swaying branches had been easy enough to spot. He knew a passing breeze hadn't gotten them moving because none of the higher branches in the trees were swaying.

The movement Ed had spotted was even tougher to explain. While some trees could very well have caught a little gust of wind that hadn't touched any of the others, the motion of the ground at the base of some of those trees was definitely peculiar. Slocum reached down into his saddlebag to retrieve his field glasses. When he put the glasses to his eyes, the lenses were pointed at a spot fairly close to where the movement had been.

"See anything?" Ed asked.

"Not yet."

"I can't see it at all anymore."

Slocum wasn't about to write it off just yet, but was beginning to think he'd lost sight of it as well. After sweeping the glasses back and forth a few times, he became convinced that he was searching the right spot. The movement was no longer there, however. "Could have been a trick of the light," he said.

"I guess so, but . . . I don't know. It ain't that bright out here."

Slocum didn't need to look away to verify that. A bank of think, gray clouds had rolled in to blot out most of the sun. While there didn't seem to be a danger of rain, the sky had been turned into the color of damp stone. It was the kind of light that filtered down through the clouds to bathe every-thing below in washed-out hues.

"Could it have been an animal?" Ed asked.

"I don't think so," he sighed. "I'm starting to think it's just some little breeze swirling around out there, kicking up dead leaves and pushing the branches around."

Ed was hesitant to reply, but he finally gave in. "I suppose. Wait!" he snapped while stretching a hand out far enough for Slocum to see a few fingers at the edges of his lenses. "Right over there. Near the right edge of the trees. I saw it again."

Because he was looking at a much narrower portion of the horizon, Slocum had missed it. He panned his field glasses over and caught sight of something moving on top of the ground. The longer he looked, the more he swore it could have been the ground itself writhing beneath a carpet of leaves at the feet of those trees. Wind rustled near the spot where he and Ed had come to a stop. Judging by the soft rustle of leaves close by, it could very well have been the same breeze that had gotten both men so suspicious. Just when Slocum was about to write the whole thing off as a couple of twitchy minds feeding off each other, he saw the motion among the trees again.

This time, it was different. Instead of something shifting beneath the fallen leaves, the leaves themselves were mov-ing. Upon closer inspection, he saw it was something cov-ered by leaves that was moving. That distinction, combined with the howl he'd heard, made whatever was crawling around out there seem much more common.

Slowly shaking his head, Slocum said, "I think it really is just some animal."

"What about that howling? I never heard the likes of that before."

"Could be a wounded animal. You ever hear a rabbit being eaten by a coyote? You'd swear it was singing."

"What I heard wasn't singing," Ed insisted. "Surely you agree with that."

"I'm not about to agree with anything. All I know is—" Suddenly, Slocum's field of vision was eclipsed by a wave of rough edges and dark browns. He was still looking through the field glasses, and when he lowered them, he saw something resembling a piece of earth that had come up to swat him in the face.

A dull, thumping impact hit Slocum in the ribs, sending him reeling back in his saddle. His ears were filled with the pounding of blood rushing through his head as well as the churning of his own breaths. The howl that had brought both men up the ridge came back. Somehow, it seemed both distant and terrifyingly close at the same time. Along with that, several voices screamed and hollered in a frenzied but very human war cry.

Ed's horse reared up and let out a loud whinny. He struggled with the reins using one hand while pulling his Smith & Wesson pistol with the other. More shapes sprang from the ground amid fluttering leaves and bits of dirt as if they'd been spat up from the earth to attack them. Slocum wasn't able to distinguish much from where he sat because he was leaning back and to the side after getting the wind knocked out of him. He collected himself in less than three seconds, but hoped that wasn't too late.

Straining to pull himself upright again, Slocum reached for the Colt at his side. Before he could get to the weapon, his arm brushed against something coarse and tough. It was the same flailing attacker that had knocked him back, and it was still swinging at him with limbs wrapped in filthy rags and layers of old, decaying leaves. The stench was that of rotten soil beneath an old, fungus-encrusted log. Bitter and sickeningly sweet, the odor clung to the back of his throat as he tried to draw his next breath. Ed struggled with more of them, but Slocum had to put that aside when he caught the glint of a blade coming at him.

He leaned back even farther than when he'd been knocked back a few seconds ago. A knife sliced through the air inches in front of him and came back again less than a heartbeat later. Slocum brought his free hand up to grab the mess of filth and leaves just below the knife. Sure enough, his fist closed around something that felt like an arm beneath that mess. He kept his grip to prevent the knife from being buried into his chest while swinging his gun around to fire a quick shot. The Colt barked once, hitting nothing. It had been his intention to buy himself some time and breathing room by startling his attacker. Unfortunately, this attacker wasn't about to be startled.

Another gunshot went off, followed by Ed's voice. "Get the hell off'a me!" he shouted.

Once again, Slocum tried to regain his balance. Just as he got his bearings, something slapped against his face to blot out the light and smother him in more of the sickening scents he'd caught earlier. Trying to breathe only made matters worse. His stomach churned and his head spun as he was not only cut off from his air, but forced from his saddle and partly off his horse.

Slocum's feet were caught in his stirrups and his horse turned around in a nervous circle. His first instinct was to fire another shot, but Slocum held off until his gun bumped against something solid. When he heard the shooting iron scrape against dead leaves, he pulled his trigger. He must have hit the attacker while that knife was being swung because Slocum felt something scrape against his chest rather than plunge straight into it. He fired again and again, hoping to discourage his attacker from cutting his throat as he dangled from the side of his horse.

Pain lanced through Slocum's leg as the foot caught within the stirrup became twisted at an odd angle. Somewhere along the line, he'd freed the foot from the right side, which didn't help him much since his entire body was slipping down along the horse's left. He couldn't even guess how his limbs were tangled, but he knew the leg that was still wedged inside a stirrup was trapped between his body and his horse's side. In a matter of seconds, bone would give way and he would be in even hotter water than he was now.

Slocum gritted his teeth, collected every bit of strength at his disposal, and straightened the trapped leg as best he could. His muscles strained, pushing him away from the horse just enough to keep his leg from snapping like a dry twig. The leaf-encrusted figure with the knife came at him again. Slocum had righted himself enough to see it a little better and met the figure with the side of his Colt before it could stab him with the blade in its hand. The figure staggered away, clearing a path for Slocum to fall from his saddle.

Even after landing on his back and shoulders, his left foot was still caught in the stirrup. While upside down, at least he wasn't about to snap in several places. He stretched out his gun hand, sighted along the top of the Colt's barrel, and squeezed his trigger. This being the calmest shot fired so far, it hit its mark and spun the attacker around in a tight circle. Slocum still couldn't see much more than a vaguely human shape covered in layers of rotten mulch. One particularly welcome sight was that of a knife flying from the figure's grasp.

Another shot was fired, clipping the figure's shoulder and sending a mess of leaves flying from its body. "Go on and git!" Ed shouted amid the metallic clatter of him levering another round into his rifle.

Slocum took advantage of the brief respite by curling his torso upward so he could pull his foot from the stirrup. The figure rustled with scurrying steps that didn't seem to be drawing closer.

When Slocum freed himself, it was a mixed blessing. His leg was no longer trapped, but felt as if it had been put through a wringer. He didn't allow any of the pain to show as he pulled the aching limb in close and propped himself up onto his other leg. Since his horse was still close, he grabbed on to the saddle horn for support. "How many more are there, Ed?"

"Two or three. It's . . . hard to tell."

"I speak of robbers and thieves. Spirit Bear is not interested in money or valuables. He leaves such things behind and any of his warriors are free to take what they want. When someone kills as many as Spirit Bear, there is plenty left behind. Money. Jewelry. Horses."

Slocum took a breath, but refrained from drawing too much poisoned air into his lungs. "How has the Army missed this?" Slocum asked as he took in the sight before him. "How can this go on without being snuffed out?"

Shifting his sharp eyes back to the sprawling camp, Hevo seemed just as transfixed by the sight as Slocum. "You must have seen much, John. Surely you know that this is a wide land and the white man's eyes are rarely focused on anything that does not serve him. Spirit Bear knows this also. He stays where the blue coats seldom go and rarely leaves anyone behind to tell his tale."

As much as Slocum would have liked to dispute that, he simply couldn't. More often than not, when there was an Indian attack, it was described more by the carnage left behind than any accurate details regarding the ones who'd committed it. For too many Army officers, one redskin was the same as another. For the ones who did know the difference, Slocum doubted they would imagine something like this in their wildest dreams. He doubted many among the local tribes would even guess something like this was going on.

"You're right," Slocum said. "I have seen a lot. Now let me tell you something else I've seen. I see those lunatics dancing around in that smoke like they were smelling daffodils. I've also seen them charge through it without faltering while men like me and Ed and Josiah could barely get our eyes to stop tearing long enough to stay in our saddles. I doubt Spirit Bear uses that smoke to control his people because his warriors fight too damn well to be out of their minds. It makes a lot more sense that they burn that smoke whenever they can so they get used to it. I've heard of

6

"What were those things?" Ed gasped.

Slocum tested his aching leg by putting some weight on it. When it didn't buckle beneath him, he tried taking a step. "They weren't things," he said. "They were men dressed up in some sort of getup so they wouldn't be seen."

"I ain't never seen men like that. Not ever!"

"That's all they are, Ed. Get a hold of yourself. Probably hunters or Indians or trappers."

A howl rolled through the air. Instead of coming at them from different angles, it rolled in from the trees like a storm. Once it reached Slocum's ears, the howl seemed to shiver and claw at him as if it were afraid of being trapped within his head.

"That wasn't made by no man," Ed said in a voice that became shakier with every word.

Slocum turned to look behind him and then around again to watch the trees. Feeling dizzier from the quick circular movements, he gripped his Colt tighter and fumbled to reload it. "Where the hell did they go? They were *just here*."

"I'm telling you, they disappeared!" Ed wailed.

"Men don't disappear."

"Those weren't men!"

After fitting the last fresh round into the cylinder and shutting it, Slocum turned on Ed and grabbed the front of his shirt. He hung on partly to rattle Ed back to his senses and partly to keep from falling over. "I saw them and they were men, damn it! They snuck up and got the drop on us, sure as hell, but they're still men and they've got to be close."

Ed was shaking his head. The rest of him started shaking when the howl rolled through the air once more.

It was a scratchy, keening sound. Slocum followed it to its source, which brought his eyes straight to those trees. He blinked away what could have been blood or sweat from his eyes, holding his gun at hip level, ready for a target to present itself. Something rustled to his right and he pivoted on the balls of his feet to aim at it. Instead of one of those leafy figures, he found only his horse. The animal was just starting to calm down after the ambush and didn't have the sense to know how close it had come to getting shot.

"What the hell's wrong with me?" Slocum grunted.

"You're lucky your leg's not busted. Or your neck, for that matter."

"That's not what I'm talking about. There's something wrong with my head. My ears. Hell, even my eyes." When the howl came again, it hit Slocum like a set of claws raking along the inside of his skull. "What is making that noise?"

"I don't know what it is . . . but I see it."

Slocum looked over to Ed and found the other man extending a shaky finger toward the distant trees.

The little bit of light that made it through the thickening layers of clouds hurt Slocum's eyes when he looked in the direction Ed was pointing. He used the pain as something to hold his focus. It was something steady and constant, unlike the swirling in his head or the slowly tilting ground beneath his feet. There was something else in those trees. It flowed back and forth like the shape he'd spotted earlier, but more so. He started walking in that direction when his boot knocked against the field glasses he'd dropped somewhere during the fight. When Slocum dropped down to pick them up, the dizziness he felt was almost enough to send him sprawling face first to the dirt. Ed grabbed one of Slocum's arms and pulled him up again.

Rather than spending the breath needed to thank him, Slocum brought the field glasses to his eyes. Gazing through those lenses made him feel as if he'd accidentally pointed them at the sun. Piercing light stabbed into his eyes, causing him to drop the field glasses quicker than if they'd been dipped into a forge.

He didn't need the glasses to see the glowing thing rise up from the ground near those trees to lift thick arms over a squat head while howling at Slocum, Ed, and the rest of the world in front of it. During the seconds when it reared up like that, the rest of the world came to a standstill. The thing's head craned back and forth as if it were howling directly at God himself.

Slocum could do nothing but watch.

Ed took a step forward, reaching with one hand while absently swiping at his eyes.

When Slocum looked toward the horses, he wasn't quite sure what he'd been expecting. Perhaps the animals would react to the sight of that thing in a different way. Maybe they could see or hear something a human being could not. But they did the very worst thing he could imagine.

Nothing.

The horses did nothing at all, apart from the normal shifting and shaking of their heads, as one might expect from an animal that was calming down after being stirred up by gunfire. Considering how much commotion had gone on around them, Slocum was grateful the horses had not bolted. On the other hand, their lack of reaction to the glowing, shifting shape out there made him feel as if he'd truly gone insane.

Perhaps thinking along those same lines, Ed asked, "Do you see that thing by them trees?"

"Yeah."

"Good."

"No," Slocum said. "I don't think there's anything good about it."

Portions of the ground rippled as though a tremor was working its way through the packed dirt or some large animals were burrowing beneath it. Compared to the sight of the tall thing with the stout head and baying howl, that wasn't so strange. What was strange was the fact that those tremors were all converging on the howling thing before disappearing from sight.

Then, the glowing thing . . . yes, Slocum had to admit to himself, the creature or whatever it was truly seemed to be glowing . . . dropped down to all fours. It turned its back to him, shambled into the trees, and was gone.

For the next few moments, Slocum remained silent. His heart slammed against the inside of his ribs and his blood raced through his veins so quickly he thought he might explode from the pressure. No matter how hard he thought about it, he just didn't know what to make of what he'd seen. Ed was silent as well until a metallic click caught their attention.

"What was that?" Ed asked.

Slocum was about to say he didn't know. Then he looked down to see he'd just thumbed back the hammer of his Colt. "That was me," he said while forcing himself to ease the hammer of the Colt back down into place. As he walked over to collect his field glasses, the pain from his twisted leg jabbed through his knee, ankle, and hip. It was better than a splash of cold water in the face to get him back on track. "Pick up your rifle."

"I . . . don't know if I can."

"Go on, Ed. Whatever it is, it's a long ways out by now."

"But where are those other things? We never saw them coming!"

Slocum pounced on him almost as quickly as the attackers had. He grabbed the front of Ed's shirt and shook him as he snarled, "You want to turn to jelly when something comes along to frighten you? Then you've got no damn business venturing past your own front porch! And if you don't pick up your goddamn rifle right now and help me find those things that bushwhacked us, you've certainly got no excuse leading those good folks down at the wagons."

Ed glanced in the general direction of the wagons as if he'd forgotten they were there. He tried to pull away from Slocum, but wasn't able to break his grip. His second attempt was much more forceful, and he turned his back to both Slocum and the wagons so he could swipe the back of his hand across his eyes.

More than anything at all, Slocum wanted to knock him onto his ass. One good punch. That's all it would have taken.

"I've got my rifle," Ed said after stooping down to pick it up.

"Now get on your horse so we can ride out to those trees." Slocum didn't wait to see if his orders would be obeyed or not. He went to his horse, grabbed the saddle horn, and climbed up. It was something he'd done so many times that he hardly had to think about it. This time, Slocum was reminded of exactly which muscles he used and what joints were bending when pain from his leg damn near set his whole body on fire.

"You all right?" Ed asked when Slocum lowered himself down and stayed put. "Need some help?"

"I'm fine," Slocum said in a sharp tone. "And I don't need any help."

Despite the warning and the daggers shooting from Slocum's eyes, Ed still wanted to help. He refrained from extending his hand all the way, however, and stayed a few steps back until Slocum was fully in his saddle. Only then did the other man climb back onto his horse.

"Come on," Slocum said before snapping his reins.

Ed fell into step a little ways behind him. From there, he shouted, "You sure we should just charge straight in like this?"

"You know where those men went?"

"No."

"Then we go where we saw them last. Something tells me they were expecting to frighten us off. If that's so, they won't be expecting us to come at them so soon."

They rode without another word passing between them. It wasn't far to those trees, but felt like several miles to Slocum's spinning head. While he wasn't dizzy enough to fall from his horse, the faster Slocum moved, the more light-headed he became. He wanted to glance back to see if Ed was having the same trouble, but was concerned that doing so might cause him to wobble even more. He'd taken knocks to the head before and knew he just had to push through until he felt better. In fact, he was feeling better by the time he pulled back on the reins and climbed down from his saddle. Of course, that could have just been the fact that his feet were once more on solid ground.

The trees loomed over them, silently watching both men who stooped beneath branches stripped bare of their leaves to inspect the ground as if worshipping at their roots. Slocum stayed on one knee as he scooped up some twigs and lifted them to his nose. "Smell that?" he asked.

"Smells like a swamp."

"Exactly. Here," Slocum said while handing over the twigs. "Smell this and tell me if it's familiar."

At first, Ed was skeptical. When he took the twigs and grudgingly smelled them, his face brightened. "Yes! It smells like those things . . . those men that jumped us. This must be where they were hiding."

Slocum picked up another twig and ran it between his thumb and forefinger. "I'm guessing this is the spot where we saw that howling . . . thing."

"You mean that spirit?"

Now it was Slocum who wore the skeptical look.

"All right, then," Ed snapped. "What would you have me call it?"

"It wasn't no spirit."

"Monster, then?"

"We don't know what it was," Slocum said definitively while straightening up and tossing the twig. "But whatever it is, it looks to be gone now. We'll ride through these trees to make sure it's gone and then head back to the wagons. Enough time's been wasted as it is."

Ed waited until they were both in their saddles before asking, "What about what that thing said? It warned us not to come here."

"We're already here," Slocum said. "Not much to be done about that now but leave and we're fixing to do that anyway."

"It probably wants for us to turn back."

Rather than twisting in his saddle, Slocum pulled hard on the reins to bring his horse around to face him. "Is that what *you* want, Ed? You want to come all this way and then turn tail and run just because some assholes jumped you? Didn't you tell me that members of your party died when you were jumped before? You lost a wagon and many of your possessions."

"I could hardly forget it," Ed snapped angrily. "And I appreciate you not talking about it as if it was some small thing."

"You and your people not only came back from that, you picked yourself up by your bootstraps and moved on when damn near anyone would have told you to stay put. That kind of gumption is part of the reason why I signed on to ride with you and yours. Hearing you talk the way you do about these crazy bandits that bushwhacked us, hearing the fear in your voice, makes me wonder if I was wise to follow you anywhere."

The anger on Ed's face slowly dissolved into confusion. "Those men, if that's what they were . . ."

"It *is* what they were," Slocum was quick to add.

"They weren't after our money. They were just out to hurt us. Maybe kill us. What purpose would be served in that?"

"Looks like they made off in this direction," Slocum said while waving toward the rest of the trees. "Doesn't look like they circled back to the wagons, though."

Ed shook his head and rubbed his eyes. "I didn't see where they went. They could be anywhere by now."

Both men brought their horses back around so they were facing the direction from which they'd come. Without another word, they snapped their reins and tapped their heels against the horses' sides.

Slocum grew more worried by the second. How could he have ridden this far, leaving the wagons behind?

Whoever those crazy, filthy attackers had been, they could very well have been meaning to draw away the wagons' protection so more men could ambush them. It was an old tactic, but if Slocum had allowed it to work, he would have a hard time looking at himself in a mirror again.

7

Slocum and Ed found the wagons trundling along on the same trail, having made about as much progress as could be expected. As the wagons shambled to a halt, he and Ed were greeted by several questions asking about the howling noises and what some had thought was gunfire crackling in the hills. Slocum kicked around the notion of saying he and Ed had frightened away some wolves by shooting at them, but knew the stranger truth would leak somehow eventually. Since it would only seem worse after having been hidden, he and Ed gave them the bare bones of the story.

"You boys got jumped, huh?" Josiah grunted once the tale had been told.

Putting on a brave face while tying his horse to the lead wagon and climbing into the driver's seat beside his wife, Ed replied, "That's right, but John and I sent them away with their tails between their legs."

"Didn't kill none of them?"

"At least one was wounded," Slocum said while tying his horse to the cook's wagon. "Probably more. I'm guessing they were just trying to spook us into offering up some sort of toll for using this trail."

Tom McCauley had been watching intently. "Did they ask you to pay a toll?"

"Not as such. We didn't give them the opportunity." Slocum sat up straight and looked at each of the anxious faces in turn. Every man, woman, and child in that wagon train listened intently when he declared, "They took a run at us and we turned them back with nothing but lead in their hides to show for it. All we need to do now is stay alert, which is what we've been doing this whole time."

"John's right," Ed told them. "This doesn't change anything. We've made it this far and we'll press on. When the next hardship comes, we'll press through that as well. Once we get to Colorado and divvy up those mining claims, we'll get together and swap stories about this journey for years to come. Tom and Josiah, you men are to take over scouting duty just like we planned. Let's all just keep doing our part and move along. Daylight's burning!"

Most of the sunlight was still being blotted out by the clouds, but some still made it through.

"What about that howling?" James Wilcox asked. Although Theresa wrapped an arm around him and whispered for him to be quiet, the skinny young boy fixed his eyes on Slocum as if the next words he spoke would be gospel.

Meeting the boy's gaze, Slocum told him, "It was just someone all gussied up to catch our attention and frighten us. That's all."

"You swear?"

"If I knew any more than that, I'd tell you."

That was good enough for James and it seemed to be good enough for everyone else. As Slocum climbed down from his saddle, Tom and Josiah climbed down from their wagons to untie horses that were kept independent of the wagon teams. After getting himself situated on his horse, Josiah looked in Slocum's direction and grunted, "Yeah.

Real good choice to bring you along. Can't think of a better way to spend our money."

"Shut your mouth, old man," Tom said as he rode to the head of the wagons. "With all the complaining you do, it's a wonder we haven't cut you loose."

Josiah laughed to himself and rode on ahead, leaving Tom and everyone else behind.

"Don't mind him," Theresa said as Slocum climbed up to sit beside her. He almost made it without a hitch, but one of his hands slipped and his weight was shifted to the leg he'd been using to climb aboard the wagon. Feeling a stab of pain through that entire side, he winced and let out a sharp breath. Theresa was right there to grab his arm and help him up. "What's the matter?" she asked. "Are you hurt?"

"Just twisted my leg, is all," he assured her.

But Theresa wasn't having it. "Come on," she said. "Follow me."

"To where?"

"The back of the wagon. I've got some blankets and a few things in there that could help you feel better."

"I don't need any medicine."

"Maybe not," she said. "But you could stand to get off that leg for a spell."

"Once I can sit down in that seat up there, I'll be off my leg just fine," Slocum insisted.

"And it'd be even better for you if you lay down and let me take a look at it."

James clambered up behind his mother to peek over her shoulder. "Go on and go with her, Mr. Slocum. My ma's a real good doctor."

In response to the question written across Slocum's face, she said, "No, I am not a doctor. I do know a thing or two about mending cuts or tending to bumps and bruises, though."

"She's real good at it," James said. "I bet she can get you feeling right as rain if you do what she says!"

"I believe my son just wants to sit up here and drive the wagon on his own, but . . ."

"But," Slocum conceded, "he does have a point. Fine. I'll get in the back so we can get moving again."

Despite his efforts to discourage her from helping him, Theresa insisted on draping one of Slocum's arms across her shoulders as if he were nursing a broken leg. Since several of the others were watching, he kept his chin up and walked as steadily as he could while loudly rebuffing her attempts to coddle him. After he and Theresa had disappeared inside her wagon, Slocum heard some snickering at what were surely lewd guesses as to what they were truly doing once that tarp had been pulled across the opening behind them.

The interior of Theresa's wagon was crammed with trunks, boxes, and a few pieces of furniture, all stacked neatly along the back and left side of the wagon. There was an area along the right side, just wide enough for someone to squeeze through if they turned themselves sideways, that she and James had been using for their sleeping quarters. Some of the boy's books and a quilt Theresa had been working on were strewn at the back of the space. She pushed all of that aside so she could reach up to pull down some of the blankets and bedding that had been stuffed on top of the crates.

"Here," she said while piling some pillows on the floor. "Lay down and put that leg up."

Slocum did as he was told. "You know," he grunted, "it's less comfortable wedging myself in here than if I was sitting up front."

She ignored that and stuffed a few folded blankets beneath his bent knee just in time to get it in place before the wagon started rolling again. "Take off that boot and let me have a look."

Once again, Slocum followed orders. His foot, ankle, and most of his calf were covered in thick, dark bruises. When she saw that, Theresa let out a hissing breath as if she was the one feeling all of that wear and tear. "What happened?"

"Got hung up in one of my stirrups," he grudgingly said. "Just like some stupid kid who's never seen the back of a horse before."

"That happened when you and Ed were ambushed?"

"Yeah."

"There was more that happened than what you told us, wasn't there?" When Slocum didn't answer, she gave his foot a quick squeeze.

"Ow!"

"Tell me the rest of what happened."

"There isn't much." Seeing that her hand was still poised above his sore foot, he quickly added, "Those men who ambushed us were strange, is all. There was a strange smell around them. I thought it was like . . ." Slocum stopped and leaned back into the folded blankets as Theresa hovered less than an inch in front of his face. "What are you doing?"

"There's something on your face."

"Like what?"

"I don't know. Your eyes are red. Looks like you're tearing up."

Slocum had felt a burning in his eyes, but hadn't taken much notice of it since his twisted leg had hurt so much. With all the wind in his face while riding and the dirt that had been kicked up in the ambush, he hadn't wasted much thought on why his eyes had been burning. Theresa, on the other hand, was much more concerned.

"Hold still," she said. Having wrapped a kerchief around one hand, she dabbed at his face and rubbed the bridge of his nose as well as his cheeks and brow. "There's something on you. Did you get any in your eyes?"

"I think it's in there now," he said. "In fact . . . damn! It burns."

"Don't rub it. You'll only make it worse."

"Can you tell what it is?"

She brought the kerchief to her nose and sniffed it tentatively. "Smells like some kind of sap. No . . . maybe some sort of glue?"

"Can't be glue. Let me see." Slocum sat up so he could smell the kerchief for himself. Although he couldn't tell exactly what it was, the scent sure brought back memories. "That's what we smelled around those bushwhackers," he said as he slumped back into the makeshift bed. The scent was weaker than before, but very distinctive.

"Stop trying to rub at those eyes," she said.

Slocum would have insisted that he hadn't done any such thing, but felt her fingers wrap around his wrist to pull his hand away from where it had been poised above his face. At that moment, he couldn't help thinking back to the times when he'd seen Ed doing that very same thing after the ambush. At the time, he'd thought Ed was fussing with a scratch or had gotten so rattled that his emotions had gotten the better of him. But Ed hadn't been cut in the face and he sure wasn't the sort to cry like a baby when things took a turn for the worse. In fact, Slocum was starting to feel badly for considering those possibilities where Ed was concerned.

"Do you have a mirror?" he asked.

"Somewhere in here, I do," she replied with a shrug. "But somewhere in here, I've got just about one of everything. What do you want a mirror for?"

"To see if there's more of that stuff on my face."

"I'm not about to root through everything just for that. Sit still," she told him as she scooted in closer to him. "I'll take another look."

She braced herself with one arm on either side of him and leaned in close enough for Slocum to feel the warmth of her body, the soft touch of her breasts against his chest, and the delicate brush of her hair against his cheek. The more he resisted the urge to kiss her, the more difficult that task became. Finally, he gave in to the urge by placing a hand on the back of her head and drawing her closer so he could press his lips against hers.

Theresa responded out of instinct. Her arms wrapped around him as best they could considering the awkward way he was propped up on all those folded blankets. Her body pushed in even closer to him and she tilted her head to an angle that allowed her to kiss him even deeper. When Slocum opened his mouth, she was quick to follow suit and the first to slip her tongue against his lips.

They might have gotten even more carried away if she hadn't accidentally dug her knee into his aching leg while trying to straddle him. When Slocum turned his head away and grunted in pain, she winced and covered her mouth.

"I'm so sorry," she said through her fingers. "Did I hurt you?"

"No . . . just . . . just get off my leg."

She crawled off as quickly as she could to sit beside him on a crate of books and papers. Placing a comforting hand upon his chest, she rubbed him and said, "I didn't mean to. I shouldn't have . . ."

"It's all right," he said. "I'm the one who started it. Did you see any more of that stuff on me?"

She laughed quietly. "Actually, I wasn't looking for it. You startled me and I got a bit swept up. Here . . . let me take another look."

When she closed in on him this time, she did so as if she was trying not to break him. Her hands were placed on either side of his head and she examined him with calmer, more scrutinizing eyes. Even then, Slocum couldn't help taking a moment to admire her beauty.

"There's streaks of it here and there," she said. Her fingers wandered along his ears and through his hair. Before Slocum could make sure she was still on task, she told him, "There's a lot more back here. Didn't see it before because your hair was covering it and it mixed with some dirt and such. Let me get you cleaned up."

Using some water from a canteen, she wet the kerchief and proceeded to wipe away the trail dust as well as the stuff that had been smeared on him. "Whatever this is," she said while rubbing vigorously at the side of his face, "it's sticky. Almost like tar or some kind of syrup."

"That'd be the worst-tasting syrup I ever heard of," Slocum said.

"It sure would. I imagine it must feel pretty good to get this stuff off of you."

"It does. I'm feeling a lot better than before. You were right about putting this leg up."

"I'm amazed you rode all the way back with that kind of injury. I knocked my shoulder out of joint once and nearly passed out from the pain. Even after it was put back right again, I was still dizzy for a few hours."

"This wasn't nearly as serious as that," Slocum told her.

Ever since the wagons had gotten moving again, Slocum and Theresa had been rocked back and forth within the confined space. The boxes and furniture around them creaked or groaned every now and then, but had been packed too tightly for them to worry about it falling over. As she looked down at him, the wagon rolled over a particularly deep rut in the trail that knocked her off her balance. He took advantage of the moment by wrapping her up in his arms once more and pulling her on top of him. Since she was lying mostly on her side, there was no danger of her inadvertently jabbing his leg.

"If I talked harshly to you when I was climbing into the wagon," Slocum said, "it was just for the benefit of the others."

"Oh. So everyone else benefited from watching you act like an ass?"

He laughed and settled into the bed a bit more. "I can only imagine what everyone was saying after they heard that howl and saw me and Ed ride off the way we did."

"We've been through a lot since we all left our homes,

John. We've seen and heard worse than that. When the wagons caught fire and Peter Bourne was caught in the flames. He . . . it was . . ." She closed her eyes and drew a steadying breath. Nestling within Slocum's embrace comforted her enough to go on. "It was terrible. But that howling . . . was strange."

"I thought so, too. I just didn't want anyone else to get rattled. Bad enough you heard the gunshots."

"Since you don't know who or what was out there, I take it those shots didn't hit anything?"

"They did. I don't know how many, but some were hit."

"And what about the howling? Just some crazy man trying to frighten us like you said?"

Slocum stared at the tarp stretched above him, but was clearly seeing more than just the thick, weathered material. "The ones that attacked us were men. They wore some sort of cloaks or something with leaves and dirt stuck to it. I didn't even get a good look at any faces, but I could feel it was a man beneath all of that mess. I couldn't check each of them. I don't even know for certain how many there were. I just don't know if I'd call them crazy."

"They sound crazy to me."

"There was a method to what they were doing. They might not have gone about things in a way I know, but they were able to sneak up on me and Ed when both of us were out there looking for anything out of the ordinary. Even now, I'd swear to the Almighty himself that there wasn't anyone in that field beforehand. They had to be out there, though. *Had* to be. They were there and they could stay hidden long enough to jump me and Ed without benefit of horses, firearms, or high ground."

"This is Indian country," she said. "I've heard of savages dressing up in all sorts of ways to stay hidden. They even paint their faces and wear feathers and such. Maybe that's all it was. Crazy Indians."

"Whole damn thing is crazy."

She settled against him and let out a slow, measured breath. "Should we be worried about this, John?"

"It's like you said, everyone on these wagons has already weathered more than one storm and you all knew there would be more to come," he said. "If threats are all it takes to change someone's mind, they shouldn't expect much of a life anyways."

"That's a fine bunch of inspiring talk," she said dryly. "I want to know an honest answer to my question. Should we be worrying about these animals or Indians or . . . whatever they may be?"

"I don't think they should be ignored, but they can't be allowed to stop us in our tracks."

"Do you think they'll attack us again?"

"Maybe. Maybe not," Slocum replied. "If I could guess what's running through their minds, they wouldn't have been able to get the drop on us in the first place." The moment those words left his mouth, Slocum regretted them. While he knew he could be franker with her than some of the others, he still didn't want to burden her with too much frankness.

He leaned forward so she could hear him as he dropped his voice to a low, intimate whisper. "I'm not just here to collect my fee. I took this job and I don't intend on letting anything happen to you or any of these folks."

"Why did you take this job? I mean, you don't strike me as a man who was just sitting around scraping together money. You're certainly not just a hired gun."

"I'm not rich, but I can afford to be particular when it comes to picking jobs. Ed seemed like a good man and my instinct told me he genuinely needed help. I was ready to refuse him several times. Even during the ride to meet up with the wagons, I was searching for a good enough reason to just refuse his offer and part ways. He spoke highly of everyone here. Well . . . everyone but Josiah."

"What did he say about him?" she asked with a laugh.

"Called him a cantankerous blowhard. Also said he was good with a rifle, though."

Theresa seemed disappointed. "We've called Josiah a lot worse than that to his face. I thought Ed might come up with something better when he was out of earshot."

"My point is all I wanted when I met up with Ed was to get out of Missouri. I could have done that on my own. I've had to fend for myself enough times. I've also seen too many good people meet bad ends on account of rotten luck or the whims of lesser men. It never did set right with me. The way I was raised, every man should pitch in and help when he can. That way, he'll earn the right to be helped when his own run of misfortune comes along."

"So you wouldn't mind doing this for free?" she asked.

"A man's also got to earn his keep." Shrugging, he added, "If he can do so while helping those in need, then that's all the better."

"There's that silver tongue again."

"Things have a way of working themselves out," Slocum said earnestly. "Just so long as you aren't stupid and do the work that needs to be done. We'll make it through this and I'll get you to Colorado. As for my silver tongue . . . you don't know the half of it."

They remained in the back of the wagon for a little while longer, doing their best to keep quiet.

8

As much as he would have liked to keep Theresa busy for hours, she only indulged him for a short time before finishing with his leg and climbing back into the driver's seat beside her son. No matter how badly his leg hurt, Slocum needed a splash of cold water more than anything else after she left him without doing much more than kissing him for a few minutes. Still, it was better than nothing.

Now that he had some time to take stock of his injury, Slocum realized how very lucky he was. Even a small sprain or any one of dozens of lesser pains could have made his job a whole lot harder to do. As it was, years of being in the saddle and the ability to keep his wits about him when things went to hell had served him well. His leg would ache for a while, but wouldn't prevent him from doing his part on the journey into Colorado. He spent another hour or two with his leg up before getting to his feet and stretching it when the wagons stopped to water the horses. When it came time for them to move on again, Slocum got back into his saddle to take his spot riding alongside the others.

As they continued westward, Slocum kept his eyes fixed

on the horizon. Before long, his neck ached more than his leg simply because he continued to look all around for any hint of trouble or signs that the scouting party might need help. His ears strained for echoes of gunfire. His nose continually tested the winds for that sickly sweet stench from the crazy Indians who'd ambushed him and Ed.

Having thought of little else all day, Slocum convinced himself that the bushwhackers had been Indians after all. They weren't anything like the Pawnee or Cheyenne he'd met before, which didn't mean a whole lot. The tribes may live differently, look different, and speak in different tongues than the white man, but they were similar in many ways as well. They had their rules. They had their traditions. They had their ways of conducting themselves, and no matter how savage the Army or bounty hunters might swear they were, the Indians were not crazy.

There was always the possibility that those bushwhackers were something new within a particular tribe or some newly born tribe in itself. Slocum could piece that together if they crossed paths again. And if they never saw those filthy, marauding, howling lunatics again . . . all the better.

As the wagons rolled forward, Slocum's horse trotted beside them, going just a little faster than the teams. When he made it to the front of the train, he rode ahead a little ways, veered off to the other side of the trail, and slowed down so the wagons could roll past him. That way, he essentially rode in a wide, lazy circle around them all so he could get a look at all sides of the wagons while stretching his horse's legs. He was just allowing the wagons to catch up to him again when he heard May Warren call out from the front of the train.

"See anything interesting, John?" she asked.

"Franco has been peeling potatoes and carrots ever since we broke camp," he said. "I'm guessing there'll be some kind of stew for supper. That's about the most interesting thing I've seen for a while."

"Better than what I've had to keep me occupied. This one hasn't stirred since you got back." She reached over to slap Ed's shoulder. Her husband was beside her in the driver's seat, but had both feet propped up, his hat down over his face, his hands folded across his stomach, and was snoring with every breath.

"This trail's been full of more holes than a sieve," Slocum chuckled. "I'm surprised his hat wasn't knocked off or his teeth wasn't knocked loose by now. The fact that he's still asleep boggles the mind."

"He can sleep through just about anything. Seen any sign of Tom or Josiah?"

"Not yet. They're not due for another hour, though."

"It's been quiet all day long. That is," she added as she reached up to draw her shawl around her a little tighter, "after you and Ed got back from those hills."

"Quiet's not such a bad thing, you know."

"Usually not."

Slocum could tell by the way she spoke that May had plenty more on her mind that she wasn't putting into words. Rather than trying to guess what was bothering her, Slocum took a lower road. He drew his pistol, thumbed back the hammer, and fired a round into the air.

The sound of the shot cracked and rolled across the flat land in every direction, sending a nervous ripple through the horses and causing every head in the wagon train to pop up for a look. More important, Ed sat bolt upright so quickly that his hat flew from his head and his eyes snapped open.

"Wha . . . what was that?" Ed sputtered. "Who shot at us? What's goin' on?"

"I thought I heard some kind of wild boar taking a run at us," Slocum said.

Ed forced his eyes open and reached for his rifle. "A boar? What? Did you say a boar?"

Slocum holstered his Colt and scratched his chin. "On second thought, it was just you snoring. I could've sworn it was either a big ol' pig grunting or we were passing a saw-mill. I didn't see any mill, so I went with the second guess. Sorry about that."

For a moment, everyone in the wagons was dead quiet. Then, May started to laugh.

"Where's my damn hat?" Ed growled.

"It's on a horse's ass," Slocum replied.

"What was that?"

Slocum pointed at the team pulling Ed's wagon. Sure enough, when Ed had sat up, he'd pitched his hat off and it had landed on the backside of the horse directly in front of him.

May laughed even harder, causing everyone else to join in.

Ed tried to stretch an arm out to reclaim his hat, but it was just outside his reach. More than that, it seemed to have landed so perfectly upon the horse's rump that it wasn't about to be shaken off by anything short of a powerful gust of wind. Staring at the hat perched in that inopportune spot, Ed had no choice but to join in on the laughter himself. He brought the wagons to a halt just long enough to get his hat, and when they were rolling again, everyone was in higher spirits.

Once they'd resumed their former pace, Slocum heard a scratchy, nasal voice come at him like a sharpened stick poking him in the ear.

"That was a damn fool thing to do," it said.

Slocum glanced over to find a long, pale face staring back at him. "You think so, Vera?"

Vera McCauley was a sickly little thing who fought so as not to allow her ailments to get the better of her. So far, Slocum didn't even really know what was wrong with her. In fact, he didn't know what was wrong with Tom McCauley for marrying such a grating, disagreeable woman and drag-ging her across the country. Most men he knew would have gone to those lengths just to get away from her.

"I *do* think so, Mr. Slocum," Vera said. "You could have started a stampede firing a shot for no good reason like that."

"These horses are around when we hunt. We also fire shots to signal to each other from a distance. Are you trying to tell me the animals know I fired just to wake up Ed and will be upset about it?"

"I'm saying you could have spooked one of them. Isn't it bad enough you startled my children?"

Her son, Michael, poked his head up from where he'd been huddled beneath the wagon's seat. "I wasn't frightened, Momma. It was funny."

Slocum smiled over at the boy. "Thanks, Mike."

"His name is Michael," Vera snapped.

The four-year-old climbed out from where he'd been hiding, crawled onto his mother's lap, and stared at him with wide green eyes. "Can I see your gun?"

Without hesitation, Slocum drew it from his holster and started emptying the cylinder into his hand. "Of course you can, little man."

More color flushed into Vera's face than Slocum had seen since he'd first been introduced to her. "He most certainly *cannot!*" she declared. "I won't have my little boy playing with guns."

"It's not loaded, ma'am. Besides, it's not like he hasn't seen one before. Might as well take some of the mystery out of it."

"That gun of yours has caused enough commotion, Mr. Slocum, and I'm not just referring to the one in your holster. Don't think for one moment that we're ignorant of what you and Theresa Wilcox get up to."

"What does he and Miss Wilcox get up to, Momma?" Michael asked.

Just then, the flap of the wagon's tarp was pulled aside so Vera's daughter could stick her head out. "Who's getting up to something?" she asked.

Vera closed her eyes and said, "Nobody is getting up to

anything. Michael, you can hide under the seat or you can sit next to me properly. Elsie, you need to get back to your reading. Both of you need to be quiet."

Slocum raised an eyebrow and fit the bullets back into his Colt. "Seems like I'm not the one stirring things up around here."

"Hi, Mr. Slocum!" Elsie chirped. "That was real funny what you said about Mr. Warren's hat being on a horse's a—"

"Elsie!" Vera snapped. "Enough."

The girl's smirk was so wide, it seemed to cover most of her face as she slowly eased back into the wagon. Michael was also grinning while he hunkered down and lay beneath the driver's seat in a little ball.

"Do you have anything else in mind for disrupting our day, Mr. Slocum?" Vera asked. "Perhaps you'd like to make some more noise and draw more attention to us?"

"Is that what this is about? You think I made enough noise to draw attention?"

"Could be why those savages attacked you and Ed earlier," she said smugly. "Ever think of that?"

"You haven't ventured much past your own front porch, have you? Because if you did, you'd know that any Indians guarding their lands would have no trouble spotting a bunch of slow-moving wagons rolling down a trail that's probably been used by plenty of other wagons headed the same direction. All the scouting runs we've made and the campfires we've built have attracted plenty of other attention. In fact," Slocum added, "I'd be willing to listen if you had an idea of how a group this size could make it to Colorado without attracting any attention. If you don't have anything so useful to say, perhaps you should set a good example and be quiet yourself."

"That was very rude!"

More for the sake of the children listening and less for any sense of propriety where Vera was concerned, Slocum said, "Yes it was, ma'am. My apologies." He knew his point had been made. He could see as much judging by the annoyed expression on the woman's long face.

Now that she'd stopped talking, Slocum could hear the distant rumble of hooves. If not for the fact that he'd been straining to hear something along those lines all day, the sound may have been lost beneath the constant grind of wheels against the ground and the horses plodding along to keep them moving. These hooves were moving a lot faster and they immediately put Vera McCauley at the bottom of his list of concerns.

Slocum rode away from the wagons toward what he guessed to be direction he needed to go to meet the approaching horses. Expecting Tom and Josiah to be returning from scouting, he was surprised to spot three horses instead of two. He reached into his saddlebag and dug out the field glasses to take a better look.

"What's wrong, John?" Theresa called out.

"Someone's coming this way."

Ed signaled for the wagons to come to a stop, and by the time they did, the three horses were close enough for everyone to see them. "Who's that?" Ed shouted from the lead wagon.

Still staring through the field glasses, Slocum replied, "It's the scouting party."

"But I count three of 'em."

"I know. Tom and Josiah aren't alone."

"Who's with them?"

Slocum returned the field glasses to his saddlebag and removed the rifle from the boot of his saddle. "Don't know who it is. We'd best get ready to meet them properly."

Nobody in those wagons needed to be told to keep their heads down and mouths shut.

9

The wagons remained still as Slocum and Ed waited for the three horses to arrive. Both men had rifles to their shoulders and were sighting along their barrels. Ed searched the horizon for any hint of movement, including strange tremors in the ground or anything at all that might mean someone was trying to circle in on them from another angle. Slocum kept his aim on the third horse he'd spotted. Through the field glasses, he'd picked out Tom and Josiah. The other rider was unfamiliar, and even though he seemed to be accompanying the other two more or less peacefully, Slocum wasn't about to take any chances.

Once he was close enough, Josiah shouted, "What the hell's goin' on over here? I swore I heard a shot fired!"

Slocum could feel Vera's accusing stare boring a hole straight through the back of his head. "Wasn't anything," he said without giving her the satisfaction of looking back. "Who's that with you?"

Tom and Josiah rode on either side of the third man, who was an Indian with sunken features and skin that looked more like dried rawhide stretched across a wire frame.

72

Wide, dark eyes were cast downward and he kept his hands clasped around a tuft of his horse's mane. He had no saddle and no gun. In fact, the only thing he did have was a set of buckskin britches and a shirt made of tanned skins still bearing the coarse hair of the animal from which it had been taken.

Josiah held his pistol in one hand and reached over to grab the Indian's shoulder. "We found this one poking around on a ridge less than a mile from this here trail," he said while pulling the other man upright. The Indian rode bareback, but still seemed to be better situated on his horse than the men on either side of him. "Ain't that right, boy?" Josiah sneered.

No man, regardless of where he came from, appreciated being treated like something less than an animal. Even if the Indian didn't know a word of English, the tone in Josiah's voice had more than enough disgust in it to convey his meaning. Slocum guessed the Indian to be somewhere in his late twenties or early thirties. Whichever it was, he was old enough not to take kindly to being called a boy.

"Did he attack you?" Slocum asked.

"Not as such," Tom replied.

Before the larger man could explain any further, Josiah said, "Didn't have to attack us! He was creepin' around, skulking behind us, dogging our trail like some goddamned rodent."

"So if he didn't attack you," Slocum said, "that means he's only guilty of riding in your vicinity?"

Although he didn't put anything to words, Tom gritted his teeth and sighed. More than likely, he'd made either this same argument or another very similar one not too long ago. It seemed Josiah was as closed to suggestions now as he ever was.

"I don't need nobody to tell me when to be suspicious of someone!" Josiah growled. "I know sneaking when I see it and this here redskin was trying not to be seen while he followed Tom for more'n three miles! If Tom hadn't had his head in the sand, he would've seen as much for himself."

"I saw plenty," Tom said in his own defense.

"You didn't see this one until I fired a shot at him."

"What was he doing that you shot at him?" Slocum asked.

"He was creepin' on the ground, comin' up on fat Tom here, while he was takin' a piss!" Josiah said. "After what you told us about crazy men jumpin' up from the ground and comin' at you with knives, I figured I shouldn't be too careful. He even smells bad, just like you mentioned in your story."

Slocum approached the three men, sliding his rifle into the saddle's boot so he could skin his Colt instead. As he got closer to the Indian, he watched for any sign of hostility. All he could gather after closing the distance between him and the dark-skinned rider was that the Indian could very well be a bit older than Slocum had guessed. There didn't seem to be any immediate threat, especially since he could now tell that the Indian's hands were tied together by a rope around both wrists. The other end was tied to Josiah's saddle horn.

"It was more than just a story." After pulling in a deep breath through his nose, Slocum added, "And this man doesn't smell anything like what I smelled when me and Ed were attacked."

Josiah shrugged. "Honest mistake. Every Injun smells like dung anyhow."

"Shut your damn mouth," Slocum said. "And if this man didn't do anything to warrant being trussed up like this, you'd best untie him."

"How do we know he won't do anything once he's free?" Josiah asked.

Slocum holstered his Colt but kept his hand resting upon its grip. "If the three of us can't do anything against one man, then I doubt we have much chance of getting all the way to the Rockies."

There was a challenge wrapped up within that logic and

it wasn't lost on Josiah. He glared defiantly at Slocum while drawing a hunting knife from the scabbard at his belt. He made a point to be especially rough with the Indian as he grabbed his bound wrists and hacked through the rope tying them together. "There," he spat while throwing the rope to the ground. "You want him free so bad, he's free. Want me to fix him a nice meal as well?"

"I take it you already searched him."

"Course we did! I ain't stupid. He had a few knives on him along with a bow and some arrows."

"No gun?"

"Damn savage probably don't know what a rifle is," Josiah grunted.

Ignoring the petulant rifleman, Slocum looked to the Indian and asked, "What's your name?"

The Indian didn't respond.

"Do you understand English?"

After a few more silent moments, Josiah grumbled, "Fat load of good this is doing. We were better off without this man tagging along."

"I did not ask to be here," the Indian said, much to Josiah's surprise.

"I believe he was referring to me as the tagalong," Slocum said. "What should we call you?"

The Indian pressed his lips into a tight line and sat so his back was straight as a board.

Josiah jammed his knife back into its scabbard and rode toward the wagons. "I call him your problem, Slocum. You need any help, you know where to come crying for it."

"What about you, Tom?" Slocum asked. "Care to tell me more about where you found this man?"

The big fellow squirmed in his saddle. When he looked toward the Indian, he reflexively pulled his reins in the opposite direction. "Just like Josiah said. He was creeping around. Josiah said he saw someone following me, and when we doubled back to have a look . . . there he was."

"I was not hunting you," the Indian said.

Slocum looked over at him. "Is that a fact? What were you hunting?"

"Spirit Bear."

"Beg your pardon?"

The Indian moved his head about a fraction of an inch so he could look Slocum squarely in the eyes. Something about the slow, deliberate nature of that motion seemed eerie. "I hunt Spirit Bear."

"Then why follow me?" Tom asked.

First, only the Indian's eyes moved toward the fat man. Then his head turned just enough to allow him to meet Tom's nervous gaze when he replied, "I followed you because Spirit Bear will come for you before anyone else. You ride like a herd of wild buffalo and you wheeze louder than wind through the branches. Spirit Bear hunts trespassers in lands he has claimed as his own because he sees it as his duty. His warriors would hunt one such as you for sport."

A sweat broke out on Tom's forehead.

"Why don't you go see your wife, Tom?" Slocum said. "I know she's worried about you."

The big man couldn't leave fast enough. He was so rattled that he wasn't concerned with appearing otherwise. Before his horse could get too far away, Ed called out from the wagons.

"Need a hand, John?"

"Not just yet."

"How long are we to stay here?"

"Go ahead and get the wagons moving," Slocum replied. "I'll bring our guest along."

"You all right on your own?"

"I'm not on my own, Ed. If this one does anything foolish, surely one of you can keep him from escaping or getting too close to the wagons."

It took a few minutes for Tom and Josiah to get their horses tethered to the wagons, and once the men were aboard, the entire train got rolling. Slocum kept his eye on the Indian and his hand on his gun. Before the wagons could get too far ahead, he looked over to the dark-skinned man and asked, "Want to come along with me of your own accord, or do I have to tie you up again?"

The Indian took hold of the horse's mane and shifted his weight upon its back. For a second, Slocum thought he was going to make a run for it. Instead, the Indian made the slightest movement with his legs that got the horse walking forward.

Slocum fell into step beside him, careful to stay close enough to keep an eye on the prisoner yet outside of his reach in case he decided to take a swing at him with an arm or leg. "Do you have a name?" he asked.

"Yes."

"Mine's John Slocum."

The Indian glanced over at him, narrowed his eyes and said, "I am called Hevo."

"What tribe do you hail from, Hevo?"

"My people are Cheyenne."

"And where are they now?"

"Why?" Hevo asked. "Do you seek to burn them from their homes and rape our women?"

"Now why the hell would you ask me something like that?"

"Because that is what the white man does best. He burns, rapes, steals, and claims land as his own when his ancestors are not even buried here."

As much as Slocum would have liked to dispute those harsh accusations, he'd seen enough blood spilled and raging fires to know the Indian wasn't exactly out of line. "Do we look like a bunch of pillagers to you?"

Hevo turned his slow gaze toward the wagons to find several little heads poking from their hiding spots to stare back at him. The moment the children knew they'd been spotted, they quickly ducked back into hiding. "Maybe not," he admitted. "But this will not matter to Spirit Bear."

"This isn't the first time I've heard folks make up tall tales to cover their tracks. Sometimes, they make up fantastic stories to justify their actions. Fact is, I've heard some pretty frightening stories about damn near every tribe there is."

"Spirit Bear is more than just a story. He is a great warrior and he hunts on many lands."

"Well, with all the men we have riding with these wagons, I think we can handle one bear."

"There is more than just one warrior," Hevo said. "You already know this. You spoke of the scent and the bear's war cry. You have seen Spirit Bear with your own eyes."

"So there's more than one?" Slocum asked.

When Hevo turned away from him to face forward, he once again spotted the children peering at him from the wagon train. The intensity that had caused his words to hang heavy in the air was alleviated somewhat when he said, "The others are Dirt Swimmers. They are warriors who travel with Spirit Bear during his hunt. They arrive before Spirit Bear and claw at the eyes of any who might dare stand against him. They smell of rotted soil. This scent comes from the dirty water running through their veins."

"That's a hell of a story," Slocum said. "Harbingers of doom. Monsters. Hunters. I imagine some of the children in them wagons might get a thrill hearing that one. I did see those Dirt Swimmers and they did do a fair amount of clawing. I saw something else, too. The thing that was doing the howling."

"Spirit Bear glows like an emerald moon. His voice rolls like thunder."

"You make it sound like this thing is a demon or some kind of devil."

"Perhaps it is," Hevo said. Then, he looked over to Slocum and added, "Or perhaps it is just stories. I know what I have seen and I know you have seen it, too. Those men who tied my hands . . . they see nothing more than what is directly in front of their noses."

"You got a point there." Leaning over a bit, Slocum asked, "Why did you let them capture you?"

"You think I allowed men like those to capture me?"

"The alternative would be that Josiah and Tom happened to get the drop on you all by themselves. They aren't incapable, but you were out there on your own and it sounds like you were pretty well armed. That means you must know how to handle yourself. Seeing as how you rode out by yourself, that says even more about your skill with the weapons that were taken from you. If you weren't by yourself," Slocum continued, "then there are others out there who didn't take a stand when you were brought in. These wagons are anything but silent, and if you had partners out looking for you, they would have found you by now."

"Perhaps they will find me now that they have followed me back here."

"So we're back to me having to believe any Cheyenne hunter would need such a ruse?"

Hevo nodded quietly. "I did think for a moment that you would believe such a thing. The men who tied my hands would have. At least, the one with the narrow shoulders and ferret's face would have."

"His name is Josiah, and yeah, I guess he does kind of look like a ferret. This is Cheyenne territory, isn't it?"

"Partly. Some of these grounds are home to the Pawnee."

"And wouldn't those tribes have reason to chase away anyone coming through without permission?" Slocum asked.

"This trail has been used by white men's wagons for many years. My tribe has traded with such travelers for food and valuables. Many times, they will pay a great price for supplies they have lost before coming here. Some will pay even more for guides that will take them to lands where they are free to plant their crops and trade in peace."

"Or to steer clear of this Spirit Bear?"

"Spirit Bear belongs to no tribe," Hevo said gravely. "He

wishes to claim territory that does not belong to him. Steal from those who would go in peace. Kill those who would harm no one."

Slocum recognized the edge in the Indian's voice. It was a cold sharpness to his tone that told him more than the words themselves. "This Spirit Bear has come after you, hasn't it? Hurt someone you know?" When Hevo stared at him, Slocum pressed on. "You know an awful lot about this man, but you talk like he's not one of your own. There's more hate than fear in your voice, but both of those things are in there. Sounds to me like you owe a whole lot of loss to Spirit Bear."

"I do."

There was plenty more to that story, but Slocum knew that if Hevo wanted to tell it, he would have. He could also tell by the firm set of the Indian's jaw and the fire in his eyes that there was no way he could force the man to say anything he didn't want to say. "So I guess that only leaves one more thing."

"Just one?" Hevo scoffed.

"Why did you let yourself be brought this far? Did you see what you wanted to see?"

"I have seen your wagons for days and I knew Spirit Bear would come for you. I also thought all of the men protecting those wagons would be like the loud ones who brought me here. Men like those do not listen to quiet words and they do not believe anything a Cheyenne or Pawnee would say. If not for the women and children within those wagons, I would have left those loud men to whatever deaths Spirit Bear might inflict upon them. But those children did not ask to be brought here. Those women are not the loud ones with the guns."

"Well," Slocum said while shifting his eyes toward the wagon where Vera McCauley watched him like a hawk, "that's true for most of those women."

"If I let the loud men capture me and ask their questions, they might believe what I told them."

"And you still made it all the way back here?"

Hevo shrugged. "They did not ask any questions."

Ed broke away from the wagon train, riding the horse he'd brought along for scouting duty. He carried a shotgun, which he kept nestled in the crook of one arm until he got close enough to point it at Hevo without putting Slocum in harm's way. "What's this man doing here, John?" he asked.

"Didn't Josiah tell you?"

"He spouted off plenty, but I wanted to hear it from you."

Hevo's grim frown shifted into a partial smirk that was just big enough for Slocum to catch a hint of it. Either the Indian was acknowledging the fact that he'd been correct to write Josiah and Tom off as idiots or he was relishing the indecision written across the white men's faces.

"This man here says he saw the same thing we did," Slocum announced. "That howling lunatic with the friends covered in leaves."

Ed shifted in his saddle. "He . . . saw it, too? The more I think about it, the more I wonder if I wasn't just out of my head for a spell. Maybe I got knocked with a rock or was imagining things."

"This is part of Spirit Bear's strength," Hevo said. "He makes you doubt your eyes and ears while his Dirt Swimmers tear at you from all sides. And when he decides the time is right, he separates your head from your neck."

"Spirit Bear?" Ed asked.

"Yeah," Slocum said. "Something even the tribes are scared of. I say we listen to what this man has to say."

"Fine, but he can't come with us like that. Josiah says he bound his hands before and you cut him loose."

"That's right, and I'll—"

"Here," Hevo said while extending his arms and holding his wrists together. "The loud ones will insist on it anyway."

"Yes," Ed replied. "They sure will."

10

Even though Ed wanted to bring the wagons to a halt so he could hear what the Indian had to say, Slocum thought it best that they keep rolling. Part of his reasoning was that the hotter heads among the group would cool down a bit once they saw that Hevo didn't pose an immediate threat, and if he did, he could be contained well enough. Another part of Slocum's decision was to just keep pushing onward and get out of Spirit Bear's hunting grounds that much sooner. After all, when a man found himself in a burning house, the best course of action was to put the fire behind him as quickly as he could.

To ease everyone's mind, Hevo's arms and legs were trussed up tight and he was placed in the back of Josiah's wagon at the back of the train. Slocum brought up the rear, watching the wagon diligently so that if Hevo somehow wriggled loose, he would be seen dropping onto open ground without getting close to any of the families. He was less worried about Hevo than about Josiah trying to do away with the Indian. If the gunshot Slocum had fired as a joke hadn't reached Josiah's ears, there was no telling what he would have done to the prisoner. For that matter, since Hevo seemed to have allowed himself to be captured, there was no telling what would have happened if Josiah had tried to push what he'd thought was the upper hand.

So the wagons moved on. Hardly a word was spoken apart from what needed to be said. The children were kept out of sight. The women were given shotguns to defend themselves. The men kept their rifles where they could get to them at a moment's notice. It was as if they'd wandered into a war zone. If Slocum didn't feel his own nerves jangling inside him, he might be amused at how much dust could get kicked up by one unarmed man who was tied up like a prize calf and wedged in between a pair of cabinets inside a covered wagon.

With everyone so focused on their tasks, the wagons made good time that day. They covered plenty of ground and didn't even consider making camp until almost every trace of sunlight had faded from the sky. A fire was built and Franco emerged from his wagon to put a meal together. Slocum so rarely saw the cook that he sometimes forgot Franco was there. Seeing the man with the plump belly carrying out pots and sacks of peeled vegetables did everyone some good. Spirits were lifted even more as the scent of Franco's beef stew started drifting through the air.

Once everyone looked to be situated in what they were doing, Slocum approached Josiah's wagon. He was stopped by the rifle in the owner's hands.

"I'll have you know somethin', Slocum," Josiah snarled from behind his Winchester. "Anyone gets hurt on account of bringing that redskin along with us, their blood is on your hands."

"What are you planning on doing with that rifle, Josiah?"

"I'll put that Injun down like a damn dog if I have to. Same thing I'll do to you if that's what it takes."

Slocum locked eyes with him. "Stand aside."

Muttering under his breath, Josiah moved along to join

the women gathered around the campfire. Slocum held off before taking another step, since it seemed there were others who wanted to have a word with him.

Tom and Ed circled around the other side of the wagons, where light from the fire could barely reach them. They brandished their weapons and wore severe expressions upon their faces. "What are you doing there, John?" Tom asked.

Slocum looked down at the shotgun in Tom's hands and said, "I was about to ask you the same thing."

Stepping past the fat man, Ed held his pistol so that it was pointed at the ground. "If you mean to speak with that Indian, you shouldn't do it alone."

"Agreed," Slocum said. "But I don't intend on my conversation turning into an execution."

"We're not killers," Ed replied with a distasteful scowl. "We're just defending ourselves. If that man doesn't mean to do us any harm, I'll set him free myself. I know you've only ridden with us a short while, but isn't that long enough to not be so suspicious of our intentions?"

"I didn't think I had to worry about your intentions so much as Josiah's."

"He's just doing what's best for us as well," Ed explained.

"It's mighty easy to talk that way now. We've tied up a man in there and brought him this far. Some might call that kidnapping."

Ed's expression shifted when he heard that. Not only was he nervous about the man being held in Josiah's wagon, but the weight of the entire day's events hit him like a load of bricks. It took Tom an extra couple of seconds, but he made the same realization before long.

"Jesus," Ed sighed. "After all that happened, I guess I just wasn't thinking straight."

"I wasn't either," Slocum admitted. "Otherwise I would have stepped in a lot earlier."

"But what if that redskin does mean us harm?" Tom asked.

"I propose we decide that for ourselves right now and either help him get back to where he needs to be or hand him over to the law in the closest town."

"John's right," Ed said. "Let's get him out of that wagon and talk to him man to man."

Slocum pulled back the cover to Josiah's wagon and found nothing but a pile of ropes where Hevo should have been. He drew his Colt and climbed inside, ready for an attack from any direction. Due to the furniture, crates, and supplies stacked inside the wagon, there was barely enough room for one prisoner to sit in plain sight. Hiding wasn't much of an option.

The ropes were sticky with a wet substance. When Slocum got outside, where he had light from the full moon as well as the nearby fire, he could see the substance was dark in color and already drying. It smelled of copper, making him certain it was blood.

"John!" Ed shouted. "Get out here!"

Slocum climbed down from the wagon and drew his pistol. Ed and Tom were nearby with their weapons held at the ready. Josiah sidestepped away from the fire, his rifle already placed to his shoulder and pointed at a lone man who approached from the opposite side of the trail. "You see?" Josiah shouted. "I told you that damn redskin was dangerous!"

"He's also got his hands raised and if he'd meant to attack us," Slocum said, "he could have done it easily by now."

A rush of panic worked through the others near the fire. Slocum knew there was precious little time before someone would pull their trigger and make things turn even uglier. "Mind if we have a word with you?" he asked.

Hevo shook his head.

"Are you armed?"

Hevo stopped, lowered himself to his knees, and placed both hands on top of his head. The other three armed men rushed forward, but Slocum made certain to get to the Indian first. Once there, he placed his hands on top of Hevo's to hold them in place while the others surrounded him. His simple clothes fit tightly on him, making it easy to see he carried nothing. Even so, Ed searched him quickly and confirmed he was unarmed.

"I say we kill him anyway," Josiah said. "He's just gonna keep dogging our trail. The son of a bitch probably told them bushwhackers where to find us already!"

"They would just have to look for the wagons or our fires," Slocum said. "Besides, he could only have been free for a few minutes. I was riding behind the wagons all day long. The only time he could have slipped away was when we were making camp. You need more proof than that, check the ropes in your wagon. The blood hasn't even had a chance to dry yet."

Josiah shoved past everyone and climbed into the wagon like he was on a mission. Judging by the look on his face when he emerged with the ropes, that mission hadn't gone well. "The blood's still wet," he admitted, "but that don't prove nothin'."

"The fact that he's here now and conducting himself in a peaceful manner proves something to me," Ed said. "At the very least, it proves he deserves to be heard."

Looking at Hevo as though the other man were crawling with lice, Josiah said, "What the hell could a damn Injun have to say that's worth hearin'?"

"I know something about the demon that attacked you," Hevo said. His words were simple and straightforward, but they froze the others in their spots as surely as if the howling thing had lifted its luminescent head directly in front of them.

Vera McCauley and her son both looked over to them. Even though the boy seemed less frightened than his mother, it wasn't much of a stretch for Slocum to assume others around the fire could overhear the men's conversation. He placed a hand upon Hevo's shoulder and directed him toward a fallen log several yards from the campsite. "Why don't we take this somewhere with a bit more privacy?" Slocum said.

Tom and Ed took a seat upon one log, and when Hevo made it clear he would remain standing, Josiah pointed a shotgun at him and told him to sit.

"No need for that kind of thing," Ed said. "He knows he's outgunned." Looking to Hevo, he asked, "You hungry?"

Hevo looked at him but did not respond one way or the other.

Ed holstered his Smith & Wesson. "How about we fetch you some supper anyway? You already been through enough. Forcing you to go without while the rest of us eat Franco's stew would just be cruel. Tom, how about you fix up a plate for our friend here?"

"Friend?" Tom snapped.

"Did he harm you in any way?"

"No, but—"

"As far as you know, did he do anything other than follow you for a while when you were out riding before?" Ed asked.

Tom's eyes lowered as if he was feeling too guilty to look any of them in the face. "No."

"Then he's a friend . . . for now."

Reluctantly, Tom got back to his feet and went over to where Franco had set up his collection of pots and tin serving plates.

Everyone else but Josiah sat on one of the logs. The grizzled rifleman stood behind Hevo with his shotgun pointed squarely at the Indian's back. When Hevo twisted around to get a look at his self-appointed guard, Slocum explained, "This is just a precaution, you understand. Until we all get to know each other a little better."

Hevo nodded, turned back around, and placed his hands upon his bent knees. "I understand."

"So," Ed said in a manner that was meant to sound calm,

but came across as forced and nervous, "why did you come back after you got away?"

"Spirit Bear hunts you," Hevo said. "He hunts me. He hunts us all."

"Why?" Slocum asked. "Just because we're crossing the land he staked out for himself?"

Hevo shook his head. "Spirit Bear knows no territorial boundaries. He is a murderous demon with coyote blood running through his veins."

"What the hell's that supposed to mean?" Josiah grunted.

"The trickster," Slocum said. Locking eyes with Hevo, he explained, "Indian chiefs tell stories about a trickster spirit. It shows itself as a coyote. Isn't that right?"

"Everyone in my tribe knows about Coyote," Hevo said. "And yes. He is the trickster."

"So that means this Spirit Bear is after something other than protecting his land?"

Hevo nodded.

Nudging Hevo with the barrel of the shotgun, Josiah said, "Mind telling us what that might be?"

"I do not know why he kills," Hevo replied. "He speaks of hate for the white man, but he also has made war with other tribes as well. Spirit Bear has plagued other hunting grounds before this one. He and his Dirt Swimmers rise up in a desert or in the mountains or in a prairie and spill the blood of good people. He does not care about the color of their skin, which tribe they are born to, or even if they are merely crossing from one spot to another. He plagued the Sioux and even visited his death upon the Cherokee Nation. He burned the houses of white men's families and attacked their trading caravans, spilling their wagons onto the ground, only to leave food and weapons scattered among the bodies and dirt."

"He's got to be after something," Slocum said.

Even in the scant bit of light that made it over to them from the fire, it was plain to see Ed's face had lost a good amount of its color. "Maybe he is a demon," he said. "I saw that thing with my own eyes. You did, too, John. No man looks like that. And them others that came up from the ground. They're called Dirt Swimmers?"

"Yes," Hevo said.

"They can't be human either."

This was the moment that Tom returned to the conversation. His eyes were wide and he seemed about ready to drop the plate of stew he'd brought over from the fire. "Not human?" he gasped. "You mean it really is a spirit?"

"No," Slocum growled. "Now sit down and lower your voice, for Christ's sake!"

Back at the fire, Theresa took it upon herself to stand up and start gathering the children so they could tell stories or sing a song. Her attempts to distract them from what the men were saying seemed to be successful, but Vera bowed her head and covered her face with her hands.

"What we're talking about is a man," Slocum said loudly enough for the entire camp to hear. "He may not be the sort of man we've come across before, but he's still a man. When you add in those others that were with him, you just get a gang of men. I've dealt with plenty of them."

Slocum sat down and put his back to the fire. When any of the other men spoke after that, they didn't have to be told to keep their voice down so as not to disturb the children playing and singing nearby.

"What about what we saw, John?" Ed asked. "The way that thing glowed. The sounds it made. That wasn't nothing like any man I've ever seen."

"Have you ever been drugged?" Slocum asked.

The question caught Ed as well as Tom and Josiah off their guard. After a few quick blinks, Ed asked, "You mean like have I ever had medicine?"

"No. I mean something like opium."

"Or peyote," Hevo added.

This time, the men regarded both Hevo and Slocum with the same kind of cautious confusion.

"I had me some peyote once," Josiah said.

Ed sighed and removed his hat so he could run his hand over the top of his head. "Why doesn't that surprise me?"

Slocum looked over Hevo's shoulder at the man who stood behind him. "Do you remember how it felt? What things looked like?"

"Light hurt my eyes," Josiah said. "I fell over a few times. Didn't see no spirit animals, though."

Hevo chuckled. "Then perhaps you didn't have enough."

"My point is that those men who came up from the ground didn't attack us right away," Slocum said in a rushed tone. "At least, not to hurt us. They rubbed something on our faces. Probably trying to get it into our nose or mouth or eyes. After that, I was light-headed. Everything seemed hazy or bright or . . . just wrong. Things sounded strange. Don't you recall that, Ed?"

"I suppose I do," he said. "It was like a bad dream. Everything I saw was peculiar. Like there was always a light shining behind it. I even swore I saw some of them Dirt Swimmers coming apart at the seams."

"Whatever that slop was that they got on us," Slocum continued, "I think you got more of it in your eyes than I did. You were always rubbing at them and it looked like they were watering. After a while, I must have rubbed some into my eyes as well because I felt that same thing." Turning around, Slocum called out to Theresa. She came over wearing a nervous smile.

"Do you recall when I came back to the wagons after Ed and I were attacked?" Slocum asked.

Theresa crossed her arms and scowled at Hevo. "Is he one of the ones that attacked you?"

"No."

"Then what's he doing here?"

"It's all right. He's—"

"And why isn't he tied up?" she snapped.

"He's not going anywhere," Slocum assured her. "I just wanted to ask you a question."

"We've got plenty of questions. Like why we're taking prisoners and what we're going to do with him and what might happen if some others like him come around looking to cut him loose?"

"You and the cook come up with all that?" Josiah scoffed.

"No," she said sternly. "Franco barely pokes his nose out of his wagon unless it's to do his job. If you would have cared to take a moment to try and talk to him, you would have seen he's terrified."

"Terrified of what?"

"Stuffing everything you own into a wagon and dragging it through hostile and dangerous territory is bad enough. His wife was killed when those robbers attacked us, and when those same robbers set a torch to our wagons, most of the goods we lost belonged to him. All he's got left is his pots and pans. He can barely sleep."

Josiah impatiently waved his hand as if he were shooing away a fly. "Fine, fine. We all have our hardships. If he's so concerned about what we're doing, he can come over here and say it to our faces."

"It's me and Vera that have the concerns," Theresa said. "And we'd like to know what it is you all are talking about. Our lives are at stake, too, you know. Ours," she added in a harsh whisper, "and the lives of those precious young ones over there."

"She is a smart woman," Hevo said.

Slocum nodded and stepped up close enough to her so that he was the only thing she could see. "Yes, and she makes some good points. Maybe this moment isn't exactly the best one to keep making them."

"What did you want to ask me?"

"I wanted to know about the stuff that was on my face when Ed and I came back from being attacked."

Perplexed by the question, she told him, "I thought it was just blood and dirt. Smelled funny, though."

"After you cleaned it off of me, did you feel strange?"

At first, she looked ready to dismiss the question entirely. Then, she stopped and rubbed her fingers together as if the strange-smelling substance were still smeared on her hand. "Come to think of it, I did. I was light-headed for a while and my head hurt."

"Did you see any strange things?" Ed asked. "Did light hurt your eyes?"

"Not as such, but I remember thinking something was wrong with my ears. At the time, I just thought I was tired and rattled after all that commotion."

"She only got a little bit of it on her hands when she cleaned me up," Slocum said to the others gathered around him. "But even then, she felt some of the effects. There's your demon. It's like I was saying before, whoever attacked us was just a man leading a bunch of other men." Motioning toward Hevo, he added, "Surely he's known of hunters who could crawl on the ground and cover themselves with leaves and dirt so they blend in. Combine a few tricks like that with this stuff that made us see and hear things and you've got something that looks like a spirit."

"That . . . stuff . . ." Hevo explained, "is called Dreaming Dust. Spirit Bear is a powerful medicine man."

Looking at Hevo with renewed interest, Tom said, "You mentioned before that he was hunting you, too."

"I did," Hevo replied with a nod.

"Is that why you came back here? Because you think we'll help you track this medicine man down before he gets to you?"

Hevo slowly looked around at the people huddled in the shadows with him. "I came back because Spirit Bear needs to be tracked down . . . before he gets *all* of us."

11

There was more that needed to be said, but that night quickly proved to be the wrong time to say it. The children got restless after wolfing down their meals, and it became next to impossible to contain them. But the young ones weren't Slocum's only concern. The more that was said about Spirit Bear, the twitchier Josiah, Tom, and Ed became. Since all three of them were armed and looking for something to shoot, Slocum felt it best to disperse for the night, have something to eat, and get some rest. There was always plenty of time for worrying later.

When Hevo attempted to loosen the reins that had been put on the horse so it could be tied to a wagon, Josiah thumbed back both hammers of his shotgun. "Just what the hell do you think you're doin'?" he growled.

Without paying attention to the shotgun, Hevo replied, "This horse goes with me."

"Not no more it don't."

"If you are horse thieves, perhaps I was mistaken in thinking you deserved to be saved."

"From where I stand, you're the one that looks like he needs savin'. Leave that horse be or I'll burn you down."

"There a problem here?"

Josiah turned, visibly shocked that Ed was the one questioning him at the moment. "Yeah, there's a problem. This Injun is taking that horse."

"It's his horse. Let him have it."

"And if he don't come back?"

"I would think you'd prefer it that way."

"All right then," Josiah said. "What if he does come back? Are we taking this redskin all the way to the Rockies?"

"Just let him take his horse. It's late and I'm too tired to argue about it." With that, Ed passed between the two men, shoving aside Josiah's shotgun as he went.

Josiah made it clear he was watching Hevo closely and continued to do so even after the Indian had climbed onto his horse's back and ridden away.

Slocum watched him leave. He leaned against Theresa's wagon as Ed walked by. "You think there's gonna be a problem there?" he asked.

Without breaking his stride, Ed told him, "We got plenty of problems, John. You don't like it? You can ride away, too." He took another half-dozen steps before stopping and turning back around.

"I know," Slocum said before the other man could say another word. "It's late. We're all tired. I didn't take offense."

"Thank you, John. It's been a long day."

"Yeah. It has. And some of us still have guard duty."

Ed paused. "I could—"

"No," Slocum cut in. "You won't be any good to anyone until you get some sleep. I don't mind taking first watch."

"You sure?"

"Yeah."

"You're a good man, John. We all owe you a lot."

"Keep that in mind when it comes time to divvy up those mining shares," Slocum said.

"I'll do that, friend."

Plenty of men called others their friend. Sometimes it was a way to get on someone's good side. Other times it was because he'd just forgotten that man's name. When Ed spoke that word, Slocum knew he meant it. That went a hell of a lot longer toward making him feel he was doing the right thing by putting his neck on the line for these folks and seeing them through this strange slice of hell they'd found out in the middle of the prairie.

Slocum took his bedroll for warmth, a cup of lukewarm coffee to keep his eyes open, and a rifle to fire at anything or anyone trying to get too close to the wagons. He picked a spot with something solid to his back, stretched his legs out, and pulled a cheap cigar from his breast pocket. The cigar remained unlit for several hours until he finally rewarded himself by striking a match and touching it to the tip of the cigar.

Nothing moved out there for several hours. When he did catch some motion from the corner of his eye, it was only Tom McCauley coming to spell him. The big man had hiked his suspenders over his shoulders and hadn't bothered tucking his shirt into his pants. "Go on," he said. "I'm sure Theresa will be waiting for you."

"You think so?"

"Come on, John. It ain't like you two were foolin' anyone. Do you think it was just dumb luck that nobody came to disturb you two when you were . . . alone? Especially with all the curious little ones we got in this caravan."

"Actually," Slocum replied, "I thought it was *extraordinary* luck." He stood up and tipped his hat. "Much obliged."

Tom nodded and settled with a labored wheeze into the spot where Slocum had been sitting. "About what I said before . . . in regards to what you and that Indian had to say . . . sorry if I spoke harshly."

"I don't recall you being harsh, Tom." The truth of the matter was that Slocum hardly thought Tom McCauley was capable of being harsh at all.

"Mostly, I wanted you to know that I'm behind Ed and I'm behind you. Josiah is, too. He may say otherwise, but his heart's in the right place."

"Did you know him since before these wagons set out?"

"We were partners for six years at a little shipping company in Virginia," Tom said. "Tact never was his strong suit, but he's a good man to have at your side when things get rough. When them robbers set the wagons ablaze before you signed on, Josiah pulled my little Elsie out of the wagon we eventually lost."

"I'll keep that in mind, Tom. You gonna be all right out here?"

"Always am."

Slocum left Tom behind and didn't have to ponder his words about Josiah for very long. Despite the older man's unvarnished exterior, his intentions had never been in question. Slocum wasn't exactly the sort to give every man the benefit of the doubt or assume a fellow had a heart of gold. He wouldn't have even taken that point of view strictly because someone like Tom had vouched for him. Instead, he judged a man based on what he saw and what he heard. So far, Josiah had been a cautious fellow wrapped up in a lot of mean talk. If he ever became worse than that, Slocum knew he could put him down without much trouble. He shook his head wearily as he approached the back of Theresa's wagon.

She pulled aside the tarp and looked outside just as he was about to climb inside. "What's on your mind?" she asked.

"I feel like a tired old man with a heart of stone."

She climbed the rest of the way down, smiling warmly at him. "You don't seem like an old man to me," she whispered. When she leaned forward to get even closer to him, it was as if the gentle winds blowing across the plains had bent her body like a reed. Soft hair drifted against Slocum's face and warm breath touched his ear as a gentle hand reached between his legs. "And I don't think it's your heart that's made of stone."

"I'd say stone is a bit of a stretch there," he told her.

Taking Slocum by the hand, she led him toward a shadowy patch of tall grass about thirty yards away from the wagons. It wasn't until she was pulling him down with her to the ground that he spotted the little lean-to that had been set up in the small clearing. It was just a folded bed sheet supported by two stakes to form an angled canopy that nearly came up to Slocum's knees.

It was cold out there, but he felt plenty warm once he was lying in the grass beneath that crude shelter with Theresa wrapped around him. "Looks like you were busy while I was on first watch," he said.

"And shame on you for not seeing me when I snuck out here to set this up."

He started to respond to that, but was silenced by a fingertip placed squarely upon his lips. After that, there was no need for words. He wrapped his arms around her and she draped a leg over him. They lay side by side, kissing each other deeply and savoring a stretch of time where there was nothing else in the world to worry about.

The only howl he heard was that of the ever-present wind. Slocum had grown so accustomed to hearing it after spending so much time in the flat lands of Nebraska that he almost didn't hear it anymore. Beneath the rustle of cold, dry grass brushing against itself was the sound of Theresa pulling open Slocum's belt. Before long, he felt her hand slip into his jeans so she could stroke his penis as it became erect. It didn't take long before he was hard and ready for her.

She was ready for him as well. Not only was she missing any undergarments beneath her skirt, but her pussy was slick with moisture. Slocum rubbed the wet lips between her legs until she pressed herself against him so he could feel every one of the shudders that passed through her body. Before she climaxed, Theresa tugged Slocum's jeans down and rolled him onto his back. She then crawled on top of him, straddling his hips and keeping her face within an inch of his so as not to knock over the lean-to.

They still didn't say a word to each other. Theresa merely looked down into his eyes while reaching down for his cock and guiding it to where it so desperately needed to be. Her eyes closed and a contented sigh escaped her lips as he entered her. Slocum ran his hands along her sides, feeling the slope of her breasts through the material of her blouse while pumping up into her. They swayed freely with the steady motion of his thrusts, and when he let up for a moment, she rocked back and forth to keep the momentum going.

His hands settled upon the generous contour of her backside. Giving in to his instinct and desires, he grabbed her tight to thrust vigorously into her once again. Her eyes snapped open and an excited breath caught in her throat. She dug her fingers into the ground and pressed her lips against his to keep from accidentally crying out.

After she'd caught her breath, Theresa propped herself up a bit so she could stare down into Slocum's eyes. She gripped him tight between her legs and moved her entire body in a slow, urgent rhythm. He could feel her hard nipples through the material of her blouse as her breasts brushed against his chest. Keeping his hands on her hips, he could feel every motion of her body as she rode him. The sound of her barely contained breaths mixed with the hushed nighttime noises all around.

Slocum closed his eyes and savored the way she felt. Her slick pussy lips eased up and down along the length of his shaft, making him harder. When his pole became more rigid inside her, she rode him even harder. He eased his hands up along her body until they were touching her breasts. As he massaged them, Theresa propped herself up a little more.

He opened his eyes to get a look at her. She still had hers closed with an expression of pure concentration. She reacted to every sensation he gave to her. And when he pulled open her blouse to fondle her bare breasts, she smiled and craned her head back until it touched the interior of the lean-to. Slocum thought about rolling Theresa over so he could climb on top of her, but she wasn't about to relinquish control. In fact, she placed her hands flat upon his chest and sat upright so she could pin him to the ground while grinding on top of him.

From this angle, Slocum was given a real good look at her swaying breasts. Her small nipples were fully erect and she sucked in a quick, excited breath when he teased them between his fingers. She settled down to take every inch of him inside. Slocum began pumping his hips to push even deeper, which caused her eyes to flutter open as if she'd been caught by surprise. Her breaths came in short bursts and she placed one hand on his stomach as if to steady herself. With her other hand, she held on to Slocum's arm in a grip that was strong enough to leave a bruise.

As Theresa shifted her hips to move his cock within her, Slocum moved his hips as well. The climax that swept through her sent a shudder beneath Theresa's skin that he could feel when he reached up to pull her down close. One hand was on the back of her head so her face was tight against his neck, and the other hand reached down to caress the smooth curve of her backside.

Theresa could barely move and she wasn't about to try. Her orgasm was just fading as Slocum exploded inside her. He pumped up into her again and again as his pleasure rolled through him in waves. When it subsided, all he could do was release his grip on her and allow his arms to fall to his sides.

She lay on top of him for a short while, occasionally shifting her weight to savor the feel of him still inside her. Eventually, she eased onto her side and lay beside him. Slocum thought he could fall asleep in that spot, but knew that wouldn't be easy to explain to any curious little faces that might find them. Just when he'd thought Theresa may have drifted into an exhausted slumber, he felt her hand slip between his legs.

"Might want to give me a minute or two," he whispered.

"I just like to touch you."

Her hand lingered where it was for a short while and then she helped him ease back into his jeans. It didn't take much for her to button her blouse and pull her skirt back in place. After that, they stayed under the lean-to and watched the sky.

They would have to get back to the wagons soon, for the sake of appearances as well as being safe from animals or whatever other dangers might prowl the prairie at night. For now, however, Slocum and Theresa enjoyed the quiet, cool darkness.

12

The following morning was almost as quiet as the previous night. Franco got up before everyone except the man on watch duty and brewed a pot of coffee while frying up some cuts of salted bacon. He scrambled some eggs and added chopped peppers, which he considered to be a plain, almost sorry excuse for breakfast. Slocum forgot all about sleeping in his bedroll on the ground near the fire when he caught the scent of that bacon. By the time he'd fixed himself a plate, several others were making their way out of the wagons or from the other bedrolls that had been scattered on the ground near the fire.

Even the children were quieter than normal. Their heads remained cast downward, only to be raised when seeking occasional assurances from parents that were busily glancing along the horizon for silhouettes of unwelcome visitors. Nobody mentioned the topic that had dominated the previous night's discussion, but it was obvious that everyone was thinking about Spirit Bear. If the strange hunter had wanted to weaken the wagon train by sowing seeds of fear and anxiousness among its members, he'd done one hell of a good job.

As Franco was cleaning up and everyone else was preparing to get moving again, a horse rode in from the north. All eyes fixed upon that horse, and when it got within range, Josiah and Ed pointed their rifles in its direction. The rider came to a stop and raised his hands.

"Lower your guns," Slocum said while stepping forward. "It's Hevo."

Although Ed was quick to respond, Josiah kept his Winchester where it was. "He's not even armed," Ed reminded the older man.

"Still don't mean he ain't dangerous," Josiah replied.

Slocum walked by him and slapped the rifle down. "We've already been through this. Just stay here and I'll go have a word with him."

Hevo slowly approached the wagons, meeting Slocum a bit closer than the halfway point. "Are we to hunt together or not?" the Indian asked.

"We are. Will you be needing your weapons?"

Twisting around to show Slocum his back, Hevo pointed to the blades kept there by a leather strap crossing his chest. "Already have them."

"When did you get those?"

Hevo smirked. "The old man speaks loud, but not as loudly as he snores. Tell him if I wished him harm, I could have easily slit his throat when I came back for my weapons in the night."

"If anyone asks, why don't we tell them I gave them to you?" Slocum said while leading the way back to the wagons. "I doubt he'll take much comfort from what you said."

"As you wish."

"By the way . . . what else did you see when you were sneaking around here last night?"

Hevo looked over at Slocum with a sly grin on his face. The grin didn't tell Slocum enough, however, to let him know if it was there because of taking the weapons out from under Josiah's nose or if he might have seen anything involving Slocum and Theresa. The Indian replied, "I came only for the weapons," which still didn't put Slocum's question to rest.

Deciding to let the matter drop, Slocum approached Ed and Josiah. Both men came out to meet them with their rifles held in a low grip.

"So did this one come by for some grub?" Josiah asked.

"No," Slocum said. "He's here to ride with us in case this Spirit Bear comes back."

"I will not ride with you," Hevo announced.

Slocum turned to look back at him. "Pardon me?"

"I can do more good if Spirit Bear does not see me with the rest of you."

"What if him or one of them Dirt Swimmers is watching right now?" Josiah asked.

"Then they will still have to divide their numbers if they want to keep watching me after I leave. If they let me go or if they do not yet know I am on the same hunt, they will be taken by surprise. Either way, it works to our advantage."

"He's got a point," Ed said.

Josiah wheeled around to glare at him and say, "You always been on his side!"

"I have?"

"Do whatever the hell you want," Josiah said while throwing a spiteful wave at them. "Last time I try to be the voice of reason around here."

"Was there a first time?" Slocum asked. When nobody saw fit to answer, he shrugged and said, "Must have been before I signed on. You want something to eat, Hevo?"

After giving Hevo some food, Slocum sent him on his way and the wagons got rolling right on schedule. Before noon, the clouds parted and the sun's bright rays flooded everything in sight. The glare from the sky as well as the nip in the air gave everything a sharp edge, like a picture that had been developed in stark contrast. Slocum didn't allow himself to be lulled into a sense of security, even when the children started singing a song that had James and Michael calling back and forth to each other from their wagons.

When Tom McCauley rode back to the wagons after scouting the trail ahead, a strangely familiar howl rolled through the air. Rather than watch what Tom was doing, Slocum shifted his focus to the ground on either side of the trail. Now that he had an idea of what to look for, he was able to pick out mounds of leaves that seemed to be moving of their own accord.

"Tom! Watch yourself!" Slocum shouted. He didn't wait for a response before reaching to the boot of his saddle and drawing the rifle kept there.

Reaching for his own rifle, Tom twisted back and forth to get a look at what could have caused such a reaction. The moment he found one of the mounds of dirt and leaves, a shape exploded from it amid an earthen spray. Tom recoiled and fumbled with his rifle, but wasn't quick enough to get the weapon out before he was beset from two sides.

Yes, Slocum realized. Two sides.

He hadn't seen the second mound of shifting dirt until it had begun to rise up on the other side of the trail. While Tom was turning toward the first figure, the second was ready to attack him from behind. Slocum placed his rifle to his shoulder, took half a second to steady himself, and fired. The shot flew a bit high and to one side, due to the fact that Slocum was rushed and didn't want to risk knocking Tom from his saddle.

It was even difficult to say if Slocum's next shot hit its target. The figures covered in their leafy cloaks moved like wild animals, reaching for Tom with gangly arms and keeping their backs hunched over. Their strange behavior as well as the leaves that flew off them could have been normal or caused by hot lead. Tom fired a shot, but his rifle was pointed nowhere near its target. The panicked reaction did nothing to discourage his attackers from pulling him down from the saddle.

"What the hell are those things?" Josiah hollered as he charged toward the wagons from a different angle. The two men must have split up sometime after parting ways with the wagons.

"Those are the same ones that attacked me and John," Ed replied as he stood up in his driver's seat. His Spencer rifle was at his shoulder, and he lined up a shot before pulling his trigger.

The Dirt Swimmers had already gotten what they were after and were smothering Tom's face with some sort of rag. Slocum reined his horse to a stop, took aim, and squeezed his trigger again. This time, he knew he'd hit his mark. The Swimmer that had been coming up behind Tom was knocked away as if he'd been kicked by a mule. When that one's body landed in the dirt, three more sections of ground sprang to life.

Where Ed's gunfire had been calmly focused before, it suddenly became hurried and sporadic. Slocum could see the fear building in Ed's trembling arms and increasingly unsteady legs. When the howl drifted through the air again, this time much closer than before, his fear built to a new height.

"Damn it!" Slocum said through gritted teeth as he snapped his reins and rode toward Tom's horse. Even when everyone in that wagon train had been expecting it, Spirit Bear had still managed to scatter them like a bunch of mindless birds.

The Dirt Swimmers almost caught him off guard yet again when another mound of dirt beside the trail stood up. This one was within spitting distance of Slocum's horse, but he was on the lookout for pieces of terrain that didn't seem to belong. As he rode, Slocum adjusted his grip on the rifle so his fingers wrapped around it like a club. With one scooping downward swing, he smashed the barrel against the top portion of a leaf-covered figure. Thanks to the swing as well as the horse's momentum, the impact was enough to send the figure sailing through the air to land in a heap.

More gunshots rang out, coming from Tom, who was still firing wildly without any prayer of hitting anything apart from the ground. Having felt the effects of the stuff the Dirt Swimmers had given him, Slocum knew the big man's vision was just as clouded as his mind. In fact, when Tom spun toward the sound of an approaching horse, it seemed he might pose as much of a danger to Slocum as the attackers themselves.

After reining to a stop, Slocum swung down from his saddle and held his rifle at hip level. He fired a shot at the first Dirt Swimmer to emerge from the ground, hoping to convince the attacker to back away from Tom. Since two of the other three were coming at him, Slocum couldn't afford to wait and see if the first one had heeded the warning he'd been given.

Now that he wasn't under the influence of Spirit Bear's concoction, Slocum could see the attackers for what they were: rowdy little men wrapped up in some kind of netting made to look like the surrounding terrain. Their covering swayed as the attackers moved, sending leaves and bits of dirt in all directions. As for the men themselves, it was difficult to tell how big they were exactly since they remained hunched over. What Slocum was more concerned about were the weapons in those men's hands. Two carried pistols and the rest held foot-long blades in a grip that kept the weapons flush against their forearms. They got to Slocum in a hurry, swinging their arms so the blade snapped out at the last moment like the end of a whip.

He used the rifle to deflect an incoming blade and then followed through by bringing his elbow around in a sharp semicircle. Slocum's arm cracked against the Swimmer's head, but some of the blow's impact was absorbed by the netting covering the other man's face. Even so, the Swimmer staggered back a step before lashing out with a swing intended to open Slocum's belly and spill his guts to the ground.

Slocum hopped back to clear a path. Knowing he was too close to make good use of the rifle as anything but a large cudgel, he shifted it to his left hand and drew his Colt with the right. Even if he'd been given a dose of Spirit Bear's medicine, Slocum would have had a difficult time missing his target from such a short distance. He fired and hit the Swimmer in the chest, sending him flailing to the ground.

"You have been warned!"

The last time Slocum heard that voice, it had sounded hollow and unearthly. Now that he didn't have a peyote mixture clouding his judgment, it sounded very human indeed. He looked for the source and found a tall man about fifty yards away wearing a thick, shaggy pelt over his shoulders like it was a kingly robe. Instead of a scepter, he waved a large stick with something attached to the top. When he waved that stick from one side to another, all of the Dirt Swimmers pulled back and crouched down beneath their netting.

"I gave you a chance to turn back and instead you sullied more of my ground with your feet and wheels," Spirit Bear said.

"If you'd just step aside, we'll be on our way," Slocum said.

The man in the pelt stepped closer. He was still some distance away, but carried himself as if he were close enough to slap Slocum in the face. "You have not seen a fight yet, white man!" Then, he hollered something in a language Slocum didn't recognize. It must have been an order to charge, because that's exactly what the Dirt Swimmers did.

13

Slocum fired at the closest two Dirt Swimmers that ran at him. They sprang at him like dogs that had been cut from their leashes and reeled away when they were met by bullets from Slocum's gun. Unsure as to how badly or even where the obscured figures had been hit, Slocum ran over to Tom.

The big man wheeled around and reflexively pulled his trigger. His pistol went off, sending its round into the tops of some nearby trees. "They're everywhere!" he said to nobody in particular. "They're demons crawling up from hell!" His face was covered in the sweet-smelling paste, which meant there was no way for Slocum or any man in his right mind to know for certain what he was seeing.

"It's me, Tom!" Slocum shouted. "John Slocum! Over here!"

When he turned toward Slocum, Tom led with his gun. Fortunately, Slocum was close enough to grab the pistol from his hand before it went off again.

"Get away, John!" Tom said, seeming not to notice the fact that he'd been disarmed. He swung his arms fiercely and stared in every direction with eyes that were obviously seeing things that weren't truly there.

As a pair of Dirt Swimmers came at Slocum, he fired two quick shots. Once more, he was unsure as to whether he'd hit them or if they were simply jumping aside to get out of the way of any more incoming fire. Ed and Josiah had joined the fray by now, firing their rifles at mounds of leaves that had the rough shape of men and moved about like overgrown rodents.

Slocum reached out to place a steadying hand upon Tom's shoulder. "Tom, listen to me. Take a breath and calm down. You're only seeing—" He was cut short by a sharp jab across his face.

"I think I got one!" Tom declared. "I think I struck down one of them demons!"

Slocum followed up with a punch that caught Tom square in the jaw. His head snapped back and his arms were still flailing as he fell over.

Now that he'd dealt with one crazy man, Slocum shifted his attention to the others. Several Dirt Swimmers straightened up and threw their cloaks back to reveal muscled chests covered in thick layers of caked mud. Strange circular symbols were drawn over their hearts and stomachs. The ones with pistols fired at Ed and Josiah. Since Slocum was closer, the ones carrying blades rushed at him.

Slocum dropped the rifle so it didn't throw off his balance when he fired the Colt. It bucked against his palm, drilling a hole through the chest of the closest Swimmer. The next attacker was so fast that Slocum didn't have enough time to shift his aim before needing to defend himself. They swarmed him so quickly and with so much reckless abandon that Slocum lost track of how many there were. It was all he could do to keep from getting chopped to pieces by the blades slashing at him.

When he saw movement to his left, Slocum turned to face that direction while swinging his Colt around. The side of the pistol knocked against a Swimmer's arm and he could barely make out the pained expression on a mud-covered face before something rustled behind him. Rather than taking the time to turn all the way around again, Slocum pivoted and dropped to one knee while keeping his Colt tucked in close to his body. Slocum snapped his left arm down and under the blade that had been sailing toward the back of his neck. Deflecting the blow before it landed, Slocum fired a shot directly into the Swimmer's stomach. The bullet sent the warrior staggering away after exploding out through a messy hole in his back.

The dead man's blade landed heavily on the ground, so Slocum scooped it up and stood to face his next opponent.

In the distance, Spirit Bear raised his staff, reared back, and howled. His call was answered by a row of three men on horseback carrying long spears and rifles. A fourth horseman was a bit farther back and rode at a full gallop to catch up with the other three. They thundered in from the left side of the trail where they could hit the rear and middle portion of the wagon train. With all the commotion so far, they must have had all the time in the world to sneak up and get in position. No longer needing to sneak, the three up front sent their spears sailing through the air.

One of the spears stuck into a wheel of Franco's wagon.

The second spear passed over the wagons to land less than a foot away from Josiah.

The third ripped through the tarp covering the McCauley wagon. A second later, a child's scream pierced the air.

Now, the three riders closest to the wagons shifted to their rifles. The weapons were all decorated with charms, feathers, and bones. Slocum's intent was to deny them their hunt. Apparently, that intent was shared by the fourth rider, who'd been charging up to the other three.

Until now, it had seemed the fourth rider was another one of Spirit Bear's warriors. Once he got a little closer, Slocum recognized the horse as well as the man upon its back. Hevo rode tall and rose up as if he had stirrups instead of just strong legs to remain in position. He and the horse moved like one creature, and even when both hands were filled with a weapon, he still managed to steer his horse expertly among the other animals.

At first, the attackers with the rifles didn't respond to Hevo's presence. Perhaps they were accustomed to seeing wild-eyed Indians charging in to join them or they could have also been shocked by the sheer intensity in this one's face. When their surprise wore off, they brought their horses around to try and stop him. They weren't able to do anything but fire a few hurried shots before Hevo was close enough to strike. He carried a knife in each hand. The blades were about a foot long and curved in the middle. Hevo swung them around his upper body so the blades looked like nothing more than blurs that caught the occasional glint of light. When one of the weapons found its target, the blur was tainted by the crimson spray of blood.

One of the riders flew from his saddle, knocked backward by the impact of Hevo's blade. Slocum saw the rifle sail from the man's grasp and couldn't be sure if the Indian's hand had flown with it. Hevo's next swing sparked against a rifle, turning the barrel away a split second before the trigger was pulled. He drove the other blade straight into that man's gut while letting out a fierce war cry that rivaled Spirit Bear's howl.

Slocum let Hevo mop up those riders and shifted his attention back to the wagons. Josiah was blazing away with his Winchester, firing round after round into the dirt mounds at his feet. Ed's horse was beside Josiah, but the man himself could not be seen. When Spirit Bear howled again, everyone stopped what they were doing. Even Slocum, who had no intention of obeying the whims of a lunatic, was compelled to hold off from pulling his trigger.

"The men you have slain this day," Spirit Bear said, "will rise again! They will attack with the might of devils! They will strike you down for trespassing upon my soil!" As he spoke, a thick, greenish fog formed behind him. He raised his staff above his head, turned his back to the wagons, and strode into the smoke.

All of the Dirt Swimmers dropped down to scamper away like four-legged animals and the one remaining rider broke away from Hevo so he could gallop toward the growing, murky cloud.

The rider thundered past Slocum and the wagons. Hevo followed close behind and slowed only so he could steady his arm to throw one of his blades at the retreating Indian. Slocum heard that blade slice through the air as it spun toward the rider's back, landing with a solid thump between the warrior's shoulders. For a few seconds, it seemed the man would keep riding toward Spirit Bear's fog. Then, he toppled from the horse's back, allowing the animal to continue on without him.

"You ain't goin' *nowhere!*" Josiah shouted as he fired at the attackers.

For once, Slocum was in total agreement with him. He ran to his horse, jumped in the saddle, and knocked his heels against the animal's sides. The horse bolted forward and Slocum joined Josiah in sending hot lead into the ever-expanding fog.

The moment the first wisp of that green smoke entered his nose, Slocum knew it was something similar to the mixture that had affected him before. One sniff was all it took to make Slocum unsteady in his saddle. Suddenly, he felt as if he was going much faster than before.

Too fast.

His horse was going wild.

Slocum had a hard time seeing through the tears flowing from his stinging eyes. When he tried to aim his Colt, he couldn't even be sure if he was lifting the damn thing high enough to hit something other than the ground. There didn't seem to be an end to the smoke. The ground felt as if it was teetering beneath him. Slocum felt the whole world tilting crazily in one direction and then another. He grabbed his reins reflexively when he thought he might fall backward from his saddle. That's when he realized the smoke wasn't affecting just him.

"Josiah!" he shouted. "Can you hear me?"

"I . . . hear ya . . . damn it!" Josiah said between hacking coughs.

"We need to turn back. The smoke is getting to the horses. They're gonna throw us and bolt!"

"To hell with—"

As if responding to what Slocum said, Josiah's horse whinnied and stomped the ground. Slocum couldn't see much but he could hear the fit the horse was throwing as well as Josiah's attempts to calm it. Finally, Josiah swore and said, "Let's just get out of this damn smoke!"

Slocum followed the sound of the other horse's steps as best he could. He thought they were still mostly following their original course, but when the smoke began to clear, he saw they'd veered well away from the trail. That didn't matter, however, since Spirit Bear and his followers were nowhere to be seen.

"Where'd that damn Injun git to?" Josiah growled.

Looking around for any trace of the attackers, Slocum replied, "He knows this land better than we do. Could be anywhere."

"So you just wanna give up, then? Those savages fire at us and hurt our young ones and you just wanna let 'em go?"

"What would you rather do? Pick a direction and ride that way for a few miles, firing at nothing?"

"They must've left a trail. Let's find it!"

"We'll wait for the rest of that smoke to burn off and then that's just what we'll do."

Josiah rode up close to Slocum, holding his rifle as if he meant to use it. "Know what I think? You're scouting for them, not us."

"What?"

"None of this hell found us until you arrived," Josiah said. "Maybe you brought it with you!"

"You hear that crying? You hear those voices? That's our own people. They're hurt and scared and they're *alone*. If those Indians really want to finish off this wagon train, the best time to do it would be when the men that are supposed to be protecting it go riding off half-cocked and leave the others to fend for themselves. If you want to do that, I say it's not me who's the one putting those good people in harm's way."

Josiah chewed on those words and he chewed them hard. Every muscle in his face jumped beneath his skin. Water streamed from his eyes and nearly every pore as if something were wringing him out like a dirty rag. Before he could say anything, a familiar cry pierced the air. It was the child's cry that had erupted when one of the mounted attackers threw a spear into the McCauley wagon.

Neither man had to say another word. Both of them rode around the perimeter of the smoke and found their way back to the wagons. Theresa and Franco stood side by side, each holding a weapon. As Slocum drew closer, he could see them trembling like blades of grass in a stiff breeze.

"Who's hurt?" Slocum asked while dismounting. "Is anyone injured?"

Franco stepped forward. He lowered his shotgun so as not to point it at Slocum. "Mrs. McCauley is inside with her children. One of them was hit by a spear."

"How bad?" When Franco shook his head, Slocum turned to Theresa. "How bad is it?"

"Can't say yet, but she's putting up an awfully loud fuss. Sometimes that's a good sign."

Slocum had seen plenty of wounded people to know Theresa had a point. More often than not, the gravest wounds were the silent ones and those who suffered from them didn't suffer long. When someone was hollering, it meant they were still kicking. Even so, hearing a child holler that way wasn't an easy thing to bear. "Is that Elsie?" he asked.

"Yes," Franco said. "The poor little thing . . . she . . ."

Josiah lunged at the cook, grabbed the front of his shirt, and shook him as he snarled, "You hid inside yer goddamn wagon like a yellow dog while the rest of us were out here chasing away them savages?"

Franco didn't have the strength to meet the other man's accusing glare.

"I should kill you where you stand."

Before Josiah could make good on his threat, Theresa pointed her hunting rifle at him. "Let him go," she said in an even tone.

"Oh, you're gonna turn on us now? At least them savages got reasons to attack us. They're animals! They don't know no better! You want to take sides with a coward?"

"He's no coward," she said. "Look for yourself."

Josiah leaned to one side so he could look past Theresa. Behind her, a body lay sprawled on its back. It was one of the Dirt Swimmers, still wrapped in its netted cloak, lying in a pool of mud that had been created by the blood that had been spilled onto the dirt. One of his legs was caught in the spokes of a wagon wheel and an expression of wild fury was frozen on his painted face. His torso was blown open; the edges of the horrific wound charred in a way that marked it as having been created by a close-range shotgun blast.

Franco stopped trembling when he looked at the body. A cold, haunted look showed in his eyes, which would most likely be with him for the rest of his life.

"That one down there slipped past you men," Theresa explained. "He meant to climb up into my wagon and . . ." She couldn't finish her sentence, especially when James peeked out at her. "I was too slow to shoot him . . . maybe too frightened. I don't know. But Franco stepped in for me. He stood his ground here to hold back the ones that slipped past everyone else."

Slocum approached the cook, placed one hand on his shoulder, and said, "You did what you had to do. Just like the rest of us."

"You shot that animal?" Josiah asked while nodding toward the corpse hung up in the wheel.

Franco drew a long breath, looked down at the body, and then locked eyes with Josiah. "He's no animal," Franco said. "He's a man, and yes, I shot him."

Josiah offered his hand, but Franco didn't shake it. Instead, the cook took off his jacket and draped it over the corpse lying in the blood-soaked mud.

"Where's Ed?" Slocum asked. "Or Tom?"

"I'll look for them," Franco said.

Josiah nodded and said, "I will, too." He then climbed back into his saddle and rode to search the tall grass alongside the trail.

"May I?" Slocum asked as he approached Theresa's wagon. She nodded and stepped aside so he could pull back the tarp and look in on the skinny little boy huddled among the stacks of furniture. "You all right, James?"

The boy nodded.

"Good. Stay put until we come for you, all right?"

James had no problem agreeing to that order.

Next, Slocum went to the McCauley wagon. Little Michael watched him approach and pulled his head back inside when Slocum got too close. He whispered to his mother, and by the time Slocum took a look inside, Vera was already making her way toward the back of the wagon. Theirs had more space inside compared to Theresa's, which wasn't saying much. There was room for two narrow piles of blankets and Elsie lay on the one farthest from the opening.

"What happened to her?" Slocum asked.

Vera's face was taut with rage. Her eyes burned with hatred. When she looked at Slocum, that hate flared before quickly burning itself out. "A spear came through and caught her in the arm. She was . . ." Tears threatened to spill down her cheeks, but she forced them back through sheer will. When she spoke again, her voice was solid as stone. "She was a bloody mess, but the wound wasn't too bad."

"I heard her screaming after the attack."

"That was because I was stitching her up." Vera looked back at her little girl. Elsie was shaking with sobs that wracked her entire little body, but her eyes were bright and her face had color. "She'll be all right," Vera said.

"Can you tend to others who might need it?" Slocum asked.

"Yes. Can you find the brutes that did this to a wagon full of children?"

Looking at the spot where the spear had torn through the wagon's covering, Slocum had to use every ounce of strength to keep from letting out his own enraged howl. "First we collect ourselves and close ranks. After that, I assure you, we'll make those savages answer for what they did."

14

Slocum's eyes were still burning when he searched the grass surrounding the trail for bodies. When he found Ed lying on his back, he thought the worst. He climbed down from his saddle, ready to drag the wagon master's corpse back to his wife.

"Take your sweet time, John," Ed grunted. "Not like I'm about to go anywhere."

Quickening his pace, Slocum said, "You're alive?"

"Believe so. I don't think dead men hurt this much."

Slocum bent down to look him over. Ed's legs were bent at odd angles and a portion of his left rib cage was bloody as hell. As far as Slocum could tell, that was the worst of it. "What happened to you, Ed?"

"One of them damn little fellas with the leaf coat jumped up from nowhere and stuck me with a spear or some damned thing," he grunted while Slocum helped him straighten out his legs and sit up. Nothing seemed to be broken. "We may agree them fellas ain't demons, but they're still the most vicious cusses I ever ran across."

"I'll have to agree with you on that." Slocum proceeded

to rip away Ed's shirt so he could get a better look. His side was torn open by a gash less than an inch wide. The edges were jagged and blood seeped from the wound. Balling up the shirt, Slocum pressed it against Ed's side and called out, "Vera! Come over here and see about stitching him up."

"What about the others?" Ed asked. "Anyone else hurt?"

"We all got knocked around pretty good. One of the McCauley children took a grazing blow from a spear. Elsie. She's all right, though."

"We should'a done a better job of protecting these folks, John. We should've turned back when we had the chance."

"Don't worry about that now," Slocum said.

For once, Josiah's timing was perfect when he shouted that he'd found Tom. Ed insisted that he go and lend a hand, so Slocum left him to be tended by Vera.

Tom was right where he'd dropped after Slocum had punched him. Fortunately, none of Spirit Bear's warriors took it upon themselves to finish the big man off. Although Tom seemed to be all right as he was helped to his feet, Slocum felt bad for almost forgetting the big man was there.

"Wha . . . happened?" Tom groaned through a face that was swollen on one side.

"Looks like you took a helluva knock," Josiah said while propping him up. His head was bowed due to Tom's arm being draped across his shoulders, but he managed to grin at Slocum in a way that made it clear he knew exactly how Tom had wound up there.

Tom's eyes were bleary and red, but at least they weren't the blank, unseeing saucers they'd been when Slocum had been forced to put him down. "Last thing I recall, I was shouting something at John," Tom said. "I think I was trying to let him know where the danger was and then . . . something hit me."

"Well," Slocum said, "the important thing is that you're all right. Apart from your face, were you hurt anywhere else?"

Josiah let him go, and Tom took a few tentative steps. His knees started to buckle and his arms seemed more like thick floppy noodles, but he seemed fine otherwise. "My head's still spinning. Is that what it felt like when you had that peyote slathered on you?"

"More or less," Slocum said. "But that smoke they got burning out here was something different. Stronger."

"I can still taste it," Tom said while smacking his lips and spitting a juicy wad to the ground.

By the time they got back to the wagons, everyone was gathered outside. The children were huddled by their parents and the women tended to the wounded. Franco and Hevo stood like an armed barrier between them and the rest of the world. Slocum, Josiah, and Tom wasted no time in calming the horses and helping everyone get back into the wagons.

"We can't stay out in the open," Ed said. He was sitting on a crate while Vera finished stitching up his side. To his credit, he didn't even wince.

"And we can't stay here," Josiah added.

May stepped forward, putting one of Slocum's fears to rest since he hadn't seen her since the shooting started. "We can't stay here?" she said. "And where do you propose we go?"

"West," Ed told her. "Just like before."

She wheeled around to face her husband. Vera was tying off the last stitch, but May seemed more than ready to push the other woman aside and pluck all the stitches out one by one when she said, "We were lucky to make it through this alive. You got hurt and I don't even want to think about how much worse it could have been for poor little Elsie."

"Turning around and going back won't make us any safer," Ed argued. "Once we get into Colorado, and civilization, we'll have a home and the law to keep watch over us."

"*Civilization,*" she spat as if the word were obscene in itself. "We already *had* civilization before this."

"But not prosperity. We already discussed this, May. We've come too far to turn back now."

"We discussed it before blood was spilled."

"And you didn't think those animals were ready to spill our blood before?" Ed roared. He tried to get to his feet, but was pushed back down again by Slocum so Vera could finally finish her work.

"Fact of the matter is," Slocum said, "you're both right. What I said before, about you needing to press on, is still true. You all knew this wouldn't be an easy trip. When you folks loaded your lives into them wagons, it was an all-or-nothing bet. You see a place you'd rather make a home? Fine. Plant your roots and make a home. Otherwise, you keep going until you find your home. You tuck your tails between your legs and run back East, you'll always regret it.

"Sure," he continued. "It was easier to agree with that before today. But this is the real test. This is where you stop talking and start fighting to back up them words we said before. It was too late to turn back yesterday and it's worse than that now. You honestly think those savages won't come back even harder if they smell fear?"

"You already sold us on this much," Theresa said.

"What I mean," Slocum replied, "is that you can't go home and you can't stay here. Those men already have this terrain scouted. They've fought here, spilled blood here, picked out their favorite spots. We need to get these wagons to a safe spot. Somewhere that can be easily defended. You won't have to stay there for long, but we should get moving away from here as soon as possible."

"Once we find this spot," May said, "how long do we stay there?"

"Just long enough for us to track down Spirit Bear and convince him to let us pass."

More than a few of the others chuckled at that.

"You think you'll just sit him down and smoke a peace pipe?" Josiah scoffed.

"If that works," Slocum replied, "I'll do it."

"What if it don't?"

"I'll think of something," Slocum told him. To everyone within earshot, he said, "And if it comes down to it, I'll send that murderous lunatic to hell myself. Not just for what he did to us, but for what he and his men did to all the others like us."

"You will kill Spirit Bear?"

Everyone turned toward the man who'd asked that question. Hevo stepped forward, leading his horse by a hand placed upon its back. His face and body were smeared with war paint and blood. Some of that blood must have come from the wounds he'd picked up in the last hour, but there was so much more of it that a good amount had to have come from other men's veins.

"Yes," Slocum said. "But I'm no executioner. I'll put an end to this insanity before someone else gets hurt. If that means I have to put an end to Spirit Bear himself, then that's the way it's got to be."

Hevo studied Slocum carefully while he spoke. Slowly, he nodded. "I believe you. I will also help you."

"I'm going with you, too," Josiah said. "I seen enough for me to trust this Injun, but I was the first man hired on to protect these wagons and I ain't about to let nobody else do my work for me."

"When we find a good spot for the wagons, you're staying behind," Slocum said. "It should just be me and Hevo that goes on from there."

"The hell I will," Josiah said.

"The only reason you don't have to bury anyone right now is because you did not allow Spirit Bear to split your numbers," Hevo said. "Spirit Bear works through fear and cunning. He has also grown proud. That can lead to the end of a warrior. He will not see what happened today as a defeat. Even now, he fills his warriors' minds with fiery words and promises of victory to come."

Seeing the confusion on Josiah's face, Slocum explained, "What he means is that this savage in bear skins has gotten too big for his britches. He's grown cocky, and that makes him careless. He'll just keep coming until someone stops him. But he's got so many crazy followers that a string of attacks will be the death of us. Bushwhackers like their ambushes, and they expect to be able to hit us harder each time they come at us. I'm guessing we can take him by surprise if we go after him for a change."

"You're guessing?" Theresa asked. "Don't you think anyone's gone after him before?"

"Maybe. Maybe not. All I know for certain is that *we* never took a run at him before. Sure, this Spirit Bear may have some mighty strange tricks up his sleeve, but in the end he's just another outlaw gang leader. I've locked horns with more than my share of those."

She was clearly troubled, but did her best to keep her voice from trembling when she said, "If something happens to you, we won't know where you are. How can we send help?"

"Don't worry about that," Slocum told her. "If something happens to me, you won't be in any position to do anything about it anyway. I know what I'm getting into."

"How will you find them?"

"I know where Spirit Bear likes to make his camp," Hevo said. "I can find him again."

Slocum nodded confidently. "I'll take a look at the tracks they left behind here. We'll follow them as much as we can and we'll find those sons of bitches. I promise you."

Although Theresa wasn't going to argue any further with him, it was plain to see she wasn't happy about his decision. And she wasn't the only one.

"I still say I should go with you," Josiah groused. "I ain't about to put my life in the hands of no Injun."

"I'm the one paying your salary," Ed said. "I'm the one who hired you to protect these wagons and the good folks inside of them, and damn it, that's what you'll do. If you want to ride off and leave us here, then you can keep riding and forget about your shares in those mines while you're at it."

Although there was still a fire in his eyes when Josiah turned to face Ed, it wasn't burning as brightly as it had a moment ago. "I'm just looking out for all of us."

"So am I," Ed told him. "We can't withstand another attack like this one. If they hit us soon enough, they'll most likely wipe us off the face of the earth."

Those words hit everyone hard. Theresa clasped her hands together tight enough for her knuckles to turn white. May put her arms around her husband and held him as if she meant to protect him against anything to come. Vera got up and went to her wagon to be with her children.

The men didn't go anywhere, but were affected just as greatly.

Ed propped himself up and looked at Slocum. "I suppose you'll want to leave before the trail gets cold?"

"That's right," Slocum replied. "The sooner the better."

Shifting his eyes to Hevo, Ed struggled to get to his feet so he could stand in front of him when offering his hand. "I know you got your own reasons for going after these men, but I want to thank you."

Hevo shook Ed's hand. "Spirit Bear has harmed many. It ends now."

"That's what I want to hear. When this is over, you've got a place among us. We can't offer much, but I have some land in Colorado. I hear it's mighty pretty."

"My land is here," Hevo said.

"Then perhaps I can offer—"

"We're burning daylight, Ed," Slocum cut in. "The decision is made. We need to get moving and so do you."

Ed smirked sheepishly. "Always was bad at good-byes."

"Hopefully this isn't good-bye. We'll catch up with you as soon as we can. Do you have anyplace in mind to take the wagons?"

"I'll have to go over my maps, but I think I know some-place that should serve us well enough."

With that, the meeting was disbanded. Slocum and Ed scoured the maps he'd brought and decided on a good-sized town less than a day's ride from the trail they'd been fol-lowing. The reasoning was that the town was big enough to have some law and so far Spirit Bear didn't seem anxious to lay siege to something larger than a wagon train. Rid-ing into a town with men dressed in netting and riders roll-ing in with a smoke cloud was even crazier than what had already happened and would surely give the Army a dozen good reasons to put Spirit Bear at the top of its bounty list.

After gathering supplies and loading his saddlebags, Slo-cum bade farewell to the others with a longer farewell to Theresa. She didn't seem the least bit concerned with whether or not anyone knew her feelings for him. She just wanted to give him one more kiss before he left her sight. It was the kind of kiss that Slocum could still feel even after taking time to revisit the spot where they'd been attacked to check for any tracks that had been left behind. They weren't in short supply.

Throughout most of this time, Hevo had made himself scarce. After the plans had been made, he told Slocum he had to make preparations of his own and said he would catch up with him after he left. Although Slocum would have pre-ferred to keep the Indian close, there was no good way of stopping Hevo before he rode away. The wagons were a mile behind him when Slocum heard a horse riding to catch up to him. He slowed his pace and watched as Hevo closed the distance to come up alongside him.

"Glad you decided to show up," Slocum said.

"You thought I would not?"

"Wouldn't blame you if you'd found something better to do."

"I owe Spirit Bear a debt that can only be repaid in

blood," the Indian said gravely. "It seems I have a better chance of settling that debt with your help."

"Some of the men we left behind might not agree. They still wanted to take a straight run at Spirit Bear."

"If they did not let us go after Spirit Bear alone, I would not have come. But I understand why they want to fight. They have a debt to repay as well. If they were to try and spill Spirit Bear's blood, they would not live to see another sunrise."

"I'd have to agree with that," Slocum said.

They rode for a few moments before Slocum broke the silence. "So do you really know where to find Spirit Bear's camp?"

Hevo hesitated before replying, "I know where his last camp was. I also know the kind of ground he likes to choose for his camps. Seeing how many men are now riding with him, I also know where he cannot make camp. That gives me enough to work with."

"Sure. All those men and their horses need water, and they need space to pitch tents and set up cooking fires where they can't be seen. I take it you're familiar with this country and know some likely prospects?"

Hevo nodded. "And I take it you picked up the tracks left by Spirit Bear's riders?"

"We're following them now, but they're already splitting apart. Won't be as easy as tracking them if they stayed clustered together."

"Between the two of us, we should find him."

"Right," Slocum said.

Close to a minute passed. This time, it was Hevo who broke the silence. "You have no plan for killing Spirit Bear, do you?"

"Pointless to burden us with an involved plan when we don't even know what we're dealing with yet or what sort of terrain we're fighting on. I do have one question for you, though."

Hevo glanced over at Slocum. "What is it?"

"What sort of name is Hevo?"

"It is Cheyenne."

"I've met plenty of Cheyenne and never one with a name like that. They're usually much more of a mouthful."

The Indian patted his horse's neck. "My true name is Hevovitastamintsto."

"Now *there's* a mouthful. What does it mean?"

"Whirlwind."

After seeing him fight, Slocum wasn't surprised in the least.

15

They rode for three days. Compared to those nights huddled beneath blankets with nothing but half a sputtering fire for warmth and eating every meal cold, life in the wagon train had been one of luxury. Everything Slocum and Hevo did was for the sake of keeping from being seen. Whenever possible, they steered clear of any trail on the off chance that it was being watched. The prairie was mostly flat, but still presented challenges. Pits in the ground could trip up a horse that was going too fast. Logs or rocks covered in tall grass could break legs, twist ankles, or even snap necks if they caused a bad enough fall.

At night, neither one of them got more than a few hours' sleep. One would watch the camp, but that didn't mean the other could rest easy. Any sound could mark the approach of a killer. Every shift of the grass could be a Dirt Swimmer creeping up on them with blades in hand. If Spirit Bear's main tactic had been to instill uneasiness in his opponents, he seemed to have done a good job. But Slocum and Hevo weren't playing into their enemy's hands. They simply couldn't afford to let their guards down.

On the fourth night, they struck pay dirt. All of their diligence in keeping their heads down while covering plenty of ground brought them close enough to spot a series of fires at the base of a range of tall hills. They weren't within sight of the Rockies just yet, but the ground was swelling with higher formations like water that was churning into bigger waves with the approach of a storm.

For over a mile before reaching the hills, Hevo had insisted they dismount and continue on foot. A quarter of a mile later, he insisted they crouch down low and walk at a pace that was slow enough for their steps to remain silent as they worked their way up the sides of the hills. When Slocum asked for an explanation, he was immediately shushed. Just when his patience was wearing thin, Slocum heard a familiar voice.

It wasn't quite a howl, but was unmistakably Spirit Bear's voice raised in what some might call a song. The chants were powerful and rhythmic. As soon as they faded, several other voices answered back.

Slocum and Hevo crested the hills on their bellies, pulling themselves forward using their elbows and knees. Although the movement had become painful early on, Slocum ignored the grinding of small rocks against his kneecaps when he saw the camp that was spread out beneath him.

A central teepee was larger than any of the dozen or so others surrounding it in a clearing that was roughly oval in shape. Apart from teepees and tents that could have come from any number of Indian camps, there were also two cabins at the far end of the clearing and several wagons parked around its perimeter. It was next to impossible to get an accurate count of how many occupied that camp. While some dancing figures were on prominent display, the shadows teemed with many others. Some of the movement could have been shadows cast by swaying trees or bodies dancing close to one of the fires or torches. Past experience with the

Dirt Swimmers told Slocum that those moving shadows could just as easily be alive themselves.

Spirit Bear himself stood upon a raised platform that looked more like a pile of refuse. He treated it like a dais, standing proudly at its peak with his arms raised high. Firelight danced across the hides covering his body and the shadows made it difficult to say which skin was his own since he and his leathers were all covered in spiral symbols painted in white.

On either side of the platform, men sat cross-legged pounding on drums with bare hands, chanting to their own rhythms. Throughout the camp, figures dressed in everything from loincloths and animal skins to the netting of the Dirt Swimmers danced and waved their hands in response to Spirit Bear's voice. There were women among them who wore only painted symbols matching those upon Spirit Bear's body. One in particular straddled what looked like a kettle from which a wispy trail of smoke rose and was fanned in every direction by her gyrating body. Her arms moved like waves in rough waters, and she snapped her head back and forth to make the beads in her hair clatter noisily.

The longer he looked at her, the closer Slocum felt to the strange, exotic woman. Although he recognized the scent of the narcotic smoke, it seemed to be weaker than before. To break the spell before it took hold of him, he asked, "Is this how many Spirit Bear usually brings along with him?"

Hevo shook his head so subtly that the motion could hardly be seen. "Many more have joined him."

"Where the hell would he find so many crazies? I thought you said he didn't lead his own tribe."

"He needs no tribe. There are some who follow him because they think he can speak with the Spirit World. Most follow him to pick the meat from the carcasses left behind."

"You're telling me they're cannibals?"

Now, Hevo looked at Slocum as if he was the crazy one.

legs scraped together. There was some play in his bindings, but only due to his own flesh being pressed together enough for his bones to ache. "See, there's what I don't like. Before, you were talking as if you were on the same side as me and the folks in those wagons. You were real convincing, too. Then I hear you talk now and it's like you've decided to separate yourself from where you were before."

"I ride alone."

"That's your choice."

"It is," Hevo replied solemnly.

"When you came to our aid during that attack, it spoke volumes about who you are. Fact is, what you did to help drive those riders away is the only thing that kept me from putting you down like a mangy, double-crossing dog after the truth came out." Continuing to rub his legs together like an overgrown cricket, Slocum said, "I still don't know if I can trust you all the way, but I do know you don't have any fondness for Spirit Bear. The hate in your eyes is too strong for that. What happened to turn you against him? Must have been something mighty awful to break the spell that would inspire all that goddamn chanting."

"What I told you was the truth. Spirit Bear killed my people. Slaughtered my tribe. Broke my woman."

"Broke her?"

Hevo did not speak and his silence billowed from every pore of his body like the sickening smoke that had rolled through the camp not too long ago.

Slocum nodded. "I understand now. It's about a woman. Always about a woman."

"You must be deaf," Hevo growled. "Do you not hear what I say about my people?"

"Yes, I heard. But you didn't sound angry enough to chew through those ropes until you mentioned the woman. What's her name?"

Hevo said nothing.

assassins who drink bits of poison to become immune to it or even men who work in laundries who can damn near pour bleach on their biscuits because they've spent so many days inhaling it."

"This is not the time for so many words," Hevo said. "We will be heard."

"Above all that music and chanting? I can barely hear myself think. Or perhaps I'm just feeling the effects of that smoke rolling up into these hills? That brings me to my point, Hevo. You don't seem to be the slightest bit dizzy from breathing this air and you never seemed to waver when the wagons were attacked."

"I have been following Spirit Bear for some time. I have often breathed his smoke."

"You rode with him, didn't you?"

Hevo turned on him so quickly that he almost resembled the twitching dancers at Spirit Bear's feet.

Slocum shook his head. "Don't give me that offended look. You know that man down there."

"Of course I do. He killed several of my people. Burned them like weeds in a field."

"He's hurt some of my people, too," Slocum said. "From the times I've seen him fight, it seems he does it the same way each time. Rides in like a demon, spouting threats, slinging spears and bullets. He dresses like a demon, talks like one, kills like one. That would hardly allow someone to get to know him the way you do."

"The only reason I follow him is to kill him."

"Sure. Maybe now that's true. But what about before? What about when you were close enough to know him as something other than a demon? When you were close enough to see what he really is and how he operates?"

"I watch him because he is my prey," Hevo insisted.

Slocum shook his head again. It didn't matter how vehemently the Indian protested, his gut instincts were saying something different. "No, if you were so fired up for revenge, you would have taken it by now. You know his tactics. You breathe this garbage in the air like it was made by a cooking fire. You knew what to look for when we were searching for this camp."

"I do not ride with Spirit Bear."

"No," Slocum said. "Not anymore is what I'm guessing. Those attacks came too close to succeeding for him to need to send you in among us. That man down there," he added while stabbing a finger toward the camp that was literally crawling with dancing figures, "is too damn crazy to do something like that. I believe you when you say you want to kill him. I just don't think it was always that way."

Hevo closed his eyes and allowed his head to angle toward the ground. The chanting stopped and Spirit Bear spoke to his followers, who were too far away for Slocum to hear what was being said. In less than a minute, the chanting started up again and the Indians sang a song that wasn't quite as frenzied as the previous one. Slowly opening his eyes, Hevo looked down at the camp as if he was studying each and every figure in turn. "Your eyes see much, John Slocum."

"And my ears work pretty good, too. You would have known that much if you'd told me the truth earlier on."

"If I told you I used to ride as one of Spirit Bear's warriors, would you have listened to my words or would you have shot me where I stood?"

"I would have made a decision based on what was in front of me," Slocum said. "The problem now is that instead of a lunatic, the man in front of me is a liar. At least with a lunatic or even a killer, I know where I stand."

"If I wanted to see harm come to you or any of those in your wagons—"

"You would have had plenty of opportunity to hurt them," Slocum interrupted. "I already thought of that, which is why I didn't mention any of this earlier. Also, I was hoping you'd come clean before we got this far."

Hevo's face became stern and cold. As the Indians in the

camp below became more joyful in their song and dance, he took on more of a shadowy aspect. "You know nothing of me or why I wish to put an end to Spirit Bear."

"On the contrary, I think I do know a thing or two about why you're doing all of this. I believe every word you said about him killing someone close to you. In fact, it was probably several people close to you. Maybe an entire group of them just like you said."

"Then what does it matter what I did before?" Hevo asked through gritted teeth.

"It matters because I'm putting my life in your hands. I spoke on your behalf to Ed and the rest of them and meant what I said."

"We are here now. Spirit Bear is in front of us. If you want to bicker some more, we should find a better place to have our words."

Slocum looked at the camp and then at the surrounding hills. The music was dying down again, but the chanting was still just as loud. There could have been Dirt Swimmers creeping up on them the entire time, but that was a given over the last several days. Strangely enough, Slocum felt more secure now that he was close enough to see where Spirit Bear lay his head at night. If a man like that was going to be so cocky when he was leading an attack, he would feel damn near invincible when he was at home.

But that's not why Slocum had waited for that moment to ask the question that had been burning in his mind. Until now, he'd had his suspicions where Hevo was concerned. Surely the Indian had proven himself more than once, but Slocum had been double-crossed by plenty of men who'd gone out of their way to prove themselves to him one way or another.

Hevo also had the hatred in his eyes when speaking about Spirit Bear and he certainly had the fire of someone who was out to settle a blood debt. Slocum wanted to believe in him and he needed Hevo's help to get this far. It wasn't until they'd approached this camp, when he saw Hevo's head bobbing almost imperceptibly to the beat of the drums and his lips moving reflexively to what must have been a familiar tune, that he knew for certain. And with that certainty, Slocum felt anger. It wasn't the first time he'd been lied to and certainly wouldn't be the last. Even so, it stung worse than a hornet trapped in his bedroll.

"I suppose we've seen what we needed to see here," Slocum said. "Let's get back to the horses before they're spotted."

Hevo remained silent, but mostly out of necessity since the noise from the camp was swiftly dying down. He and Slocum crawled like snakes in the tall grass, scraping their chests, legs, and stomachs over sharp rocks, partially buried roots, and slopes in the ground itself that bent them like rope being passed through a crooked tube. It took over half an hour for them to get back to where they'd tethered their horses, and every inch they crawled, Slocum expected to be discovered by a scout on horseback or by a Dirt Swimmer crouched less than an inch in front of him. After a while, Slocum's eyes were darting back and forth in response to so many sounds that they hurt more than the rest of his body.

From this distance, the chanting back at the camp could be heard as only a roiling echo. Light from the fires was too weak to make it this far beyond the hills, leaving Slocum and Hevo in eerie darkness. The horses were just a little farther ahead. Both men got their feet beneath them, holding still for a while to listen for rustling or movement coming from any source other than the animals. Since nothing but the wind could be heard, they stood up and walked the rest of the way to the horses. Slocum kept his hand on the grip of his Colt and Hevo maintained a firm grasp on one of his long, curved knives.

The men put some distance between themselves, but not too much. As wary as they were of their surroundings, they were taking even more precautions with each other.

Slocum heard a shifting of weight against the dirt and reflexively turned toward Hevo.

The Indian responded in kind, pivoting toward Slocum while bringing the blade up over one shoulder like a pistol's hammer being cocked in preparation to fire.

They eyed each other intently for a few seconds, each knowing that one false move could result in one or both of them being killed on the spot. They'd seen each other fight enough to know they would only get one chance to come out on top of that equation.

Slocum's eyes were focused so much on Hevo, watching for him to either throw the knife cocked by his ear or make a reach for the other blade with his free hand, that he almost didn't pay attention to what his ears were telling him. When Hevo's eyes snapped toward the barely perceptible sound of rustling leaves, it was too late for either man to do a damn thing about it.

"Aw, hell," Slocum growled as figures covered in leaves and dirt rose up from where they'd been hiding.

Not only was there a Dirt Swimmer in the spot Slocum and Hevo were looking, but three others made themselves known. All of them had weapons drawn, poised to kill their prey with arrow or spear.

Slocum might have been able to get the drop on one of them, but not before the others brought him down. He didn't like having his fate resting in the hands of lunatics, but sometimes those were the cards he'd been dealt.

16

A few minutes later, Slocum and Hevo were still alive and unharmed. Both of those things were a surprise, considering how bloodthirsty Spirit Bear's men had proven to be. Even more surprising was the fact that nobody had attempted to smear any of that peyote slime onto their faces. Instead, after a few grunted words from beneath the lead Swimmer's netted cloak, Slocum and Hevo dropped their weapons. If there had been any other option that didn't involve getting killed, Slocum would have taken it. Hevo had looked over to him for a moment, possibly waiting for a signal of some kind, but Slocum gave him none.

The Dirt Swimmers swarmed around their prisoners, bound the men's hands using lengths of rope, and escorted them back to the camp.

The chanting had stopped and many of the torches had been extinguished. Smoke still hung heavy in the air, but there wasn't anything Slocum could do apart from breathe it in. His eyes burned and his head spun a bit. Other than that, he'd either gotten somewhat used to the drug or the dosage was too small to take its full effect. He looked over to Hevo. The Indian hung his head low before finally turning to meet his gaze. Obviously, the smoke didn't affect him in the slightest. The defiance in his eyes made it clear he wasn't about to apologize for it.

They were taken to the side of the camp where two cabins stood like filthy edifices left by whoever had inhabited that patch of ground before Spirit Bear had come along. The bases of the cabins were piled high with charred bits of wood. Scorch marks rose up almost as high as the roof. Shards of broken glass were wedged in the window frames, and bullet holes had been punched through every wall. A woven blanket hung in the doorway. The lead Dirt Swimmer pulled it aside and shoved the prisoners past the cracked remains of a door that hung from one hinge.

Slocum and Hevo were pushed into one corner, forced to sit down, and held at gunpoint while their ankles were bound. Then, their arms were stretched over their heads, and the ropes around their wrists were hung over rusty nails protruding from the charred wall.

"Looks like we aren't the first prisoners brought here," Slocum said after the Dirt Swimmers filed out of the cabin's single room. "Then again, I suppose I don't have to tell you that."

"I did not mean for us to be captured," Hevo said.

"I guessed as much. You had plenty of chances to stab me in the back. Of course, if you'd come clean earlier, we could have come up with a better way of getting this far."

"No," Hevo spat. "You would not have trusted me. If you hadn't killed me, one of the others would. Probably the old one with the loud mouth."

"Yeah, I could see Josiah doing something like that."

"And you would not have stopped him." Closing his eyes and leaning his head straight back until it bumped against the wall, Hevo added, "None of them would."

Slocum tested his ropes by wriggling so his arms and

"What did Spirit Bear do to her?"

Although Hevo was quaking with rage and seemed ready to explode, he somehow kept those emotions in check.

"She's not dead," Slocum said as if he was simply mulling over the clues to a riddle he'd been given. "Otherwise you would have said so. Or you would have said something along those lines. But you didn't. You said Spirit Bear broke her. Did he rape her?"

"Are you trying to torture me?" Hevo asked in a strained voice. "Is that why you ask me these things?"

"Not at all. I'm trying to find out what's driven you this far so I can know for certain if I've still got a partner or if I was just too stupid to realize I was on my own from the instant we rode away from the wagon train."

Hevo's body convulsed as every one of his muscles strained to free him. The nail from which his wrists had been hung was just high enough to stretch out his torso and keep him from gaining any sort of leverage. It was also long enough to prevent him from sliding the ropes off it. At the moment, it seemed that he wanted to gain his freedom in order to get his hands around Slocum's neck more than anything else.

"That's what I was hoping to see," Slocum said. "Now you know how I felt when I realized you'd been lying to me."

Suddenly, like a sail that had lost every bit of wind, Hevo relaxed and dangled from his wrists. "You are a strange man, John Slocum. Going so far just to prove a point?"

"Actually, I was hoping you'd break free. Since you didn't, I'll settle for making my point."

Hevo's chest rose and fell with his labored breaths. It seemed his short-lived effort to pull free had left him completely exhausted. "I would not have allowed harm to come to any of those women or children in your wagons."

"I know."

"I did not intend for us to get captured."

Slocum's eyes narrowed as he considered that claim a bit

"What did Spirit Bear do to her?"

Although Hevo was quaking with rage and seemed ready to explode, he somehow kept those emotions in check.

"She's not dead," Slocum said as if he was simply mulling over the clues to a riddle he'd been given. "Otherwise you would have said so. Or you would have said something along those lines. But you didn't. You said Spirit Bear broke her. Did he rape her?"

"Are you trying to torture me?" Hevo asked in a strained voice. "Is that why you ask me these things?"

"Not at all. I'm trying to find out what's driven you this far so I can know for certain if I've still got a partner or if I was just too stupid to realize I was on my own from the instant we rode away from the wagon train."

Hevo's body convulsed as every one of his muscles strained to free him. The nail from which his wrists had been hung was just high enough to stretch out his torso and keep him from gaining any sort of leverage. It was also long enough to prevent him from sliding the ropes off it. At the moment, it seemed that he wanted to gain his freedom in order to get his hands around Slocum's neck more than anything else.

"That's what I was hoping to see," Slocum said. "Now you know how I felt when I realized you'd been lying to me."

Suddenly, like a sail that had lost every bit of wind, Hevo relaxed and dangled from his wrists. "You are a strange man, John Slocum. Going so far just to prove a point?"

"Actually, I was hoping you'd break free. Since you didn't, I'll settle for making my point."

Hevo's chest rose and fell with his labored breaths. It seemed his short-lived effort to pull free had left him completely exhausted. "I would not have allowed harm to come to any of those women or children in your wagons."

"I know."

"I did not intend for us to get captured."

Slocum's eyes narrowed as he considered that claim a bit

more carefully. "Near as I can tell, those Dirt Swimmers found our horses and were just waiting for us to come back to them."

"If I was to bring you to this place, wouldn't I be rewarded instead of hanging beside you?"

"Could be you're still trying to gain my trust," Slocum pointed out.

Hevo's head lolled forward and then his shoulders began to jump. The sounds he made were a mix of dry, hacking coughs and some sort of wheeze. Turned out he was laughing. The expression on his face when he looked at Slocum again was almost childlike when he said, "That is funny. Why would I need your trust? What could I possibly gain by being in this cabin rather than pledging myself to Spirit Bear so I could get something to eat?"

"What's the matter? You don't think I've got a plan in the works to get us out of here, guns a-blazing?"

"I think you do, John. I also think that plan did not involve us hanging here waiting to be executed."

"They want something else from us," Slocum said. "Otherwise they would have killed us by now."

"This is true."

"So . . . what do they want?"

Hevo sighed. "See why I did not tell you about my past? You would never be able to look beyond it. You would always think I am a part of what Spirit Bear intends to do."

"Or I might just think that you know him better than I do. After all, you did ride with him for a spell."

Finally, Hevo admitted, "The only one who knows what Spirit Bear wants . . . is Spirit Bear. I did not ride with him for long, but a lifetime would not be enough to put myself into his moccasins."

"Why would you ride with him at all?" Slocum asked.

"The same reasons most men ride with him. Greed and revenge."

"Revenge against who?"

Angling his head away as if trying to hide himself from Slocum's sight, Hevo replied, "You."

"Me? I never even heard of this crazy man until—"

"You and all white men," Hevo snapped. "There are many within all tribes across this land who want to spill the white man's blood in retribution for all of ours that has been spilled. Even when I realized I was committing the same crimes by killing based only on the color of their skin, it was too late for me to change my path. I told myself blood was the only thing white men understood, but the truth is that it felt good to kill so that is what I did. I rode with Spirit Bear for only a few moons, but it was a whole other lifetime."

"Yeah," Slocum sighed. "I've had a few lifetimes like that myself."

"I should have learned how wrong I was sooner . . . before the lesson needed to be taught to me by having blood that was precious to me spilled by the animal I had sworn to follow." Despite the fact that he already hung from the nail between his wrists, Hevo somehow drooped lower.

"What happened to your people?" Slocum asked.

"Some from my tribe came looking for me. They tracked one of Spirit Bear's raiding parties after it had burned a small mining camp. After . . . *we* burned a small mining camp. The braves came for us in the night when we were riding back to the caves where we'd made camp. They attacked and tried to separate me from the rest of the group, but I saw only enemies."

There was so much sadness in Hevo's voice that Slocum could feel it almost as powerfully as if he were experiencing it.

"I had not ridden with Spirit Bear for long," Hevo continued. "The Dreaming Dust still made my thoughts rage behind my eyes and the visions appear among the people of flesh and bone. I was not told who was attacking us. Spirit Bear was there. He came to me and insisted I prove myself by killing anyone he pointed to. And . . . because my head was swimming and my heart was filled with hate . . . I did."

Slocum wanted to ask what could fill Hevo with so much hate and such a thirst for revenge. But he could think of plenty of massacres committed by the Army, lynch mobs, or people who killed Indians for any number of bad reasons.

"Spirit Bear knew who I would be raising my blade against that night," Hevo said. "He even howled with joy when the killing was finished."

"What about your woman?"

"She was among the hunters from my tribe who came for me. She did not ride with the braves when they came to Spirit Bear's camp. She was found later, and by the time she was brought to me, she was . . . broken."

"What does that mean?" Slocum asked.

When Hevo answered that question, it seemed as if the words he had to use were pieces of broken glass scraping against his tongue. "She was given so much of the Dreaming Dust that her thoughts were no longer her own."

"Is that the same stuff that's in that smoke?"

"Yes. The Dreaming Dust can be burned, put into water, or mixed into a paste. Spirit Bear has made good use of a very bad idea stolen from many tribal medicine men. My woman was given the dust in its rawest form. After that, she was no longer the woman I loved."

"Is that so?" someone said from the cabin's single door. The words echoed within the charred room.

She was a wispy reed of a thing with long hair that was so black it looked as if it had been soaked in sooty oil. Her skin was the color of cinnamon and covered in thick layers of paint that had been swirled into the circular symbols worn by many of Spirit Bear's warriors. Grabbing the edges of the doorway as if she meant to launch herself through it, she strode into the cabin with her eyes locked on Hevo. When she spoke again, it was in a native Cheyenne tongue. *"Look at me, my whirlwind, and tell me I am not more than the woman you remember."*

Hevo straightened up and bowed out his chest. *"The woman I remember would have come to her senses by now."*

"I have. You are the one who needs to be reminded of the true path."

"Pardon me," Slocum said, "but if you two would rather be alone, I wouldn't mind showing myself out."

She approached Hevo and reached out to place both hands upon his. Her lithe body was covered by a minimum of clothing. Nothing more than a skirt made from oiled skins and a tunic stitched together from more scraps of animal hide that wrapped around her flat stomach and small, pert breasts. Both pieces of clothing were ripped in several places to show parts of symbols that, as near as Slocum could tell, were painted over her entire body. Even though she was barely over five feet tall, she lorded over Hevo as if she were the master of the entire camp. *"Will you come with me, or will you die with this . . . man?"* she asked, saying that last word as if it were a joke when applied to Slocum.

Hevo said nothing.

Unlike Slocum, this woman seemed to enjoy Hevo's silence.

"You are stubborn, as always," she said. *"I want to speak with you alone. Then, it will be seen if you chose to stand with your people or the white man."*

All this time, Slocum had listened to the mostly one-way conversation to see if he could pick up on anything. Even though he'd learned bits and pieces of a few Indian languages, he wasn't concerned with a translation. Instead, he paid less attention to the words being used and more to how they were being said. Like many women, this one figured she had an ace up her sleeve just by looking the way she did and putting herself close enough for a man to smell the sweat on her skin. Even though Slocum knew she wasn't there to help, he couldn't help being attracted to her. She brought a heat to the room just as surely as if the torches outside had been relit. Warmth radiated from her body and her hips swayed slightly as she lowered herself down to speak into Hevo's ear.

Slocum didn't know what she said to him, but the way Hevo nodded, it seemed he simply didn't have the strength to resist. She smiled and backed away. Then, she looked toward the door and said something else. Two large Indians covered in spiral symbols entered the room, released Hevo's wrists from the nail on the wall, then dragged him by the arms from the cabin.

"Good riddance," Slocum grumbled. "At least now I can hear myself think."

17

Hevo was dragged outside, but started walking once he was placed upon his feet. While escorted across the camp, he kept his head down so as not to meet the curious faces that were pointed in his direction. Many of the warriors clearly recognized him and others seemed puzzled as to what he was doing there. None of them thought to impede the guards, who took Hevo all the way to one of the teepees at the perimeter of the settlement.

The teepee was small—barely wide enough for there to be more than a foot of space beyond Hevo's feet after he was tied to the central support post. His two escorts had to duck their heads while inside and even the woman was unable to stand up straight until she was less than an arm's length away from the tallest part of the shelter.

"I will tell Spirit Bear where to find you," one of the men said.

"No," she replied. "I will tell him. Just go and make sure the other one does not try to escape."

Both of the men looked at Hevo while reflexively gripping the knives slung from their belts. Only when the woman drew a dagger from her own belt did the pair of warriors decide she had the situation well enough in hand for them to leave.

"It seems you have some of these men eating from your hand, Namid."

She smiled widely enough to crack the paint on her cheeks. "It has been some time since I was called by that name."

"What else would someone call you?"

"Spirit Bear calls me Ehtla. It means warrior princess."

"In what tongue?"

"I think he made his own language," she said. "Or he stitched one together from all the others used by the tribes. When they are united, they will need a way to speak that comes from all of them but none of them at all."

Hevo let out a grunting laugh. "You have breathed in too much of the Dreaming Dust. Or do you speak about such foolish things because you know someone is listening to you?"

Climbing on top of him, Namid straddled his lap and gently dragged the tip of her dagger against his chest.

"How can you join with Spirit Bear after what he did to our people?" he asked in a voice that was close to a growl. "I still dream of their screams. Has Spirit Bear twisted you so much that you forget the sounds of all those deaths?"

"Spirit Bear only defended himself against men that would have killed him. I weep because I knew some of those men that were killed, but they left Spirit Bear no choice."

"They were part of our tribe."

"But they were also warriors and they died in battle," she replied. "For any warrior, there is no greater honor."

"They should be mourned by their people," Hevo said. "When they look upon you from their hunting grounds, they will hang their heads in shame."

"You are just swayed, my love. You have spent too much time among people who would rather bow to their white captors than rise up against them and be free."

Hevo squinted up at her, as if that might help him see any clearer. "Who are you, Namid?"

She placed her fingertips upon his lips, stopping him before he could utter another word. When she snapped her head toward the flap of the teepee, she listened as faint footsteps crunched against the ground outside. Keeping her fingers upon his lips, she leaned toward him and whispered into his ear, "I am the same woman you remember. I was . . . someone else for a time, but I am once again the Star Dancer you once knew."

Hearing the meaning of her name spoken in her voice was almost too much for Hevo to bear. Despite the smile that fought to arrive on his face, he stared at her intently and asked, "Why should I believe you?"

Instead of speaking, she kissed him. It was jarring at first and Hevo started to recoil, but in a matter of seconds he returned her kiss with passion. His arms struggled to pull free of the ropes so they could wrap around her, but were stopped short by the bonds and the post to which they were fastened. Since he couldn't embrace her, Namid held on to him even tighter. She wrapped her arms and legs around him, running her fingers through his hair and scraping her nails against his skin. "The words I spoke just now," she whispered, "were for the benefit of the men who would listen as they guard. I think they are beginning to move away from us. There are preparations to be made."

"Why . . ." Silenced once more by her fingertips, Hevo lowered his voice so only she could hear him. "Why are you still here? Why have you pledged yourself to Spirit Bear and these murderers?"

Keeping her mouth so close to his ear that Hevo could feel the warmth of her breath, she said, "It was the only way for me to survive. When I was captured, my thoughts were tainted by the Dreaming Dust. It was in the air I breathed, the food I ate, the water I drank. My thoughts were like images reflected in flowing waters. Nothing seemed real. In the middle of this storm . . ."

". . . was Spirit Bear," Hevo sighed. "I remember that storm."

There were still footsteps outside, but they were more distant now. "After a while . . . a long while . . . I became accustomed to the Dreaming Dust," she continued. "I don't even know how long it took, but I woke up. When I did, I was accepted among these animals. Spirit Bear sings of reclaiming land and punishing the white man for what he has done, but his followers are nothing but thieves and killers. They are no better than the men that Spirit Bear wants to punish."

"The white man has his outlaws and so do we," Hevo told her. "That is the nature of all tribes. Our people have good and bad among them and so do theirs. At least you saw this truth when you woke up from your dream. I did not."

Namid moved as if she wanted to silence him again, but instead caressed his mouth and writhed against his chest. "The Army killed so many of our people, so many of our friends. You were angry and Spirit Bear's words make sense to angry ears."

As much as Hevo wanted to go along with that, he simply could not. He had seen how women captives were treated by Spirit Bear's warriors. The favorites among them were kept chained like dogs and silenced by potent mixtures fed to them in every meal. Judging by the amount of symbols painted on Namid's body from head to toe, she was very favored indeed. "What have they done to you?" he asked.

She shook her head. "Not as much as they think they have done. At least, not since I have awoken from my dream. Before I became accustomed to the Dreaming Dust, even I cannot remember. I prefer to keep it that way. Since then, I allow them to dress me as a slave but I do not act like one. When a warrior or Dirt Swimmer comes to me for pleasure,

I make sure he is given a more potent mixture of Dreaming Dust which will affect even one who breathes it every day. That, along with the firewater that thieves and killers love so much, makes certain they are in no condition to pleasure themselves let alone a woman. When the fool awakes, I tell him what magnificent stallion he is and how weak I am after sharing my bed with him. It does not matter that he fell asleep before he could lay a hand on me."

"And now? Will you set me free?"

"Not yet." When he started to question her, she quickly added, "They are wary after discovering your horses so close to our camp. The warriors are scouting for others and the Dirt Swimmers crawl on their bellies like snakes peeking beneath every rock. Of all these terrible men, I think the Swimmers frighten me the most. They will crawl through fire and not make a sound if Spirit Bear asks them to."

Hevo could feel a shudder working through her, and all he could do to calm her was stretch forward to nuzzle her with his cheek. "You should only worry if these monsters do not trouble you. My greatest shame is that I was once one of them. You must know that I rode with them freely. After the Dreaming Dust no longer twisted my thoughts, I followed Spirit Bear—"

"Because you were angry," Namid quickly said. "I know why you did what you did, just as I know the man you are. That is why it was no surprise to me that you rode away. When you left, I was still not of my own mind. Otherwise, I would have followed you."

Hevo remembered the hatred in her eyes when he'd asked her to leave with him. He could still feel her angry fists pounding against his chest followed by the cold spray when she'd spat on him and called him a traitor. Now, he regarded it as a blessing that she did not remember such things and he was not about to remind her of them.

She smiled, giving him further proof that she truly had no recollection of the indignities Spirit Bear's concoctions had forced her to commit. "When I awoke," she said, "part of me wanted to die here because I knew there was nothing left for me. Why would you return to this evil place knowing that even I was lost to you?"

"I did come back for you, Namid. I also came back to put an end to Spirit Bear."

"He may be the chief among these men, but he is not the worst among them," she said with a patience in her eyes that Hevo could not begin to understand. "Spirit Bear believes he is part of a righteous war against his enemies. He believes the ancestors killed by white men speak to him."

"He is insane," Hevo snarled.

"Yes, but he is just doing what he is supposed to do. A mad dog is supposed to attack what is near and froth at the mouth. A storm is supposed to lay waste to the land below it. And so Spirit Bear is doing what he does. The men who follow," she added with a darkening expression, "follow him to their own ends. They kill and steal because they enjoy it. Spirit Bear may have a broken mind, but he is true to what he believes. The others believe in nothing. They enjoy bringing death to others and taking what they do not own. They are bloodthirsty criminals, every bit as bad as the white men who hunted our people just to cut off their scalps and sell them to whoever would pay."

"That is why I have come back," Hevo insisted. "That is why I must be set free."

"And what of the man who was with you? It seems he does not call you friend."

"He is a good man who has every right to be suspicious of me. I will free him and you will slip away from here so you are not hurt again."

She shook her head. "They are watching for a fight now," Namid whispered. "Soon, Spirit Bear will gather them and prepare to ride out on a hunting party."

"Probably to kill the people I am trying to protect, and after that, more people will fall to this insane war."

"When Spirit Bear gathers his braves, I can set you free and we can get to your friend that much easier. Until then . . ."

Hevo felt her hands busy themselves by peeling his buckskins down over his hips so she could reach inside them. "What are you doing?" he asked.

"You do not remember?"

"I do, but this is not the time."

"Right now," she said directly into his ear, "I am supposed to be convincing you to come back to Spirit Bear. I am supposed to convince you the way only I can. And if I do not think you will be convinced, I am supposed to poison your water and tell the braves to kill your friend. If the men nearby do not think I am doing what I am supposed to do, they will become suspicious."

Her touch was familiar and became urgent as she found his growing erection. After lowering his pants enough for her to stroke every inch of him, she started tugging at her own sparse clothing. Namid was too hungry for him to waste time undressing fully. Instead, she pulled aside the loincloth beneath her skirt and guided him into her. Namid placed her hands upon his shoulders and eased herself down to take every inch of his rigid pole inside herself. She leaned her head back and didn't try to stifle a moan of ecstasy.

Outside, a few gruff voices chuckled to one another and some footsteps moved closer the teepee. Hevo saw the flap pulled back, allowing one of the braves to peek inside. A warrior's scarred face cracked into a vulgar smile before finally retreating outside again.

If Namid took any notice of the leering face, she gave no indication. Her eyes remained closed and her hands had become busy peeling away the clothes from her body. The tunic she wore was pulled off and cast aside, revealing smooth, dark skin covered in the spiral symbols of Spirit Bear's tribe. She ran her hands over herself, perhaps imagining they were Hevo's, paying special attention to the hard nipples capping her pert little breasts. She ground her hips against him, moving his cock within her body until it hit the exact spot she wanted.

Hevo struggled against the ropes binding his arms and legs. Although he was aware that one of the braves could look in on them again, he still wanted to break free of the ropes just so he could get his hands on his woman. Before he could get too frustrated, he felt her touch graze against his chest and stomach. She'd opened her eyes and was massaging the flesh above his heart while repositioning herself on top of him.

She brought her legs up close so they could be bent and spread open. Squatting on top of him while holding on to his shoulders, she rode him in slow, even motions. Hevo opened his eyes, no longer struggling to break from the ropes but enjoying the wetness of her body and the way she enveloped him. When Namid leaned forward, he was able to place his mouth upon her breasts and suck on her nipples the way he knew she liked.

Some things would never change, no matter how much time had passed or how much hardship had been endured. Namid trembled when she felt her lover's lips, prompting her to ride him even harder than before. Finally, she arched her back and tossed her hair while letting out a shuddering moan. Hevo leaned against the post, grinding his hips in time to her rhythm. When he felt his cock slip out of her, he found himself struggling once more to break free and take control.

Namid watched him with a wicked little smile. She stood up and looked down at him, slowly gyrating to a song that she softly hummed at the back of her throat. Although the song could be mistaken for one of many chants, Hevo knew it to be one that she'd sung for him when their lives were simpler and they knew nothing of the troubles beyond their native lands. He wanted to sing with her as well, but found he was too distracted by the dance she performed for him.

Namid swayed her hips and allowed her hands to roam over her body, smiling as though he were the one caressing her stomach, rubbing her breasts, sliding along her hips, and easing between her thighs. She turned around and leaned her head back while stretching her arms up toward the highest point of the teepee. Just as she was about to bump against the interior of the shelter, she lowered herself down again. Although she straddled him once more, she did not squat on top of him as before. This time, she turned around so Hevo could drink in the sight of her smooth back and tight little buttocks as she went down on all fours and teased him with more carnal gyrations.

She kept her back to him, rubbing her slick pussy lips against the tip of his penis until he parted her and slipped inside. She reached between her legs to stroke him while easing him all the way inside and then stretched both arms out to claw at the dirt while rocking her entire body back and forth.

From his perspective, Hevo was treated to the delicious view of her backside as it bobbed up and down. The symbols painted along her spine and across her shoulder blades writhed as she continued to twist and stretch to the rhythm of their song. Since he could not grab her hips in his hands, Hevo did the next best thing and pumped into her. His feet pressed against the dirt floor to give him leverage so he could pound his cock between her legs with growing intensity.

When he touched the sensitive spot inside her, Namid held her position and turned her head around to look back at him. Sweat glistened upon her brow and her voice started to tremble. Finally, she could no longer hold back. She crawled forward, stood up, and drew the dagger that still hung from the thin strip of leather wrapped around her waist. Climbing on top of him, she reached around and cut the ropes encircling Hevo's hands.

No matter how badly he wanted to be free so he could

exact his revenge, Hevo had more important matters to tend to. The instant his hands were loose, he grabbed her face and pulled her close enough to kiss. Namid pulled away, but only to cut the ropes binding his ankles before being swept up in his arms. He grabbed her roughly, held her in place, and gnawed on her like an animal. She smiled widely, turned back around, and opened her legs. Hevo wasted no time in grabbing her hips and pumping into her from behind.

After only a few powerful thrusts, Namid cried out as a powerful orgasm rushed through her body. Hevo gripped her tightly and pounded into her again. It wasn't much longer before he cried out as well and pressed his cock as deeply into her as it could go. By the time his pleasure had waned, he felt even more light-headed than when the Dreaming Dust had had its grip on him.

Less than a minute passed, barely enough time for the two of them to catch their breath, before the same brave poked his head into the teepee. He found Hevo sitting with his back against the post and his legs stretched out in front of him. His hands were clasped behind his back and out of sight. The few pieces of clothing Namid wore were draped across his ankles, hiding them.

"Will he join us?" the brave asked.

When Namid smiled, it was the same cruel smile she'd shown Hevo when she'd been pretending to be under Spirit Bear's sway. "I have reminded him of what he has missed."

The brave nodded and looked at Hevo as he would look down at a rabbit caught in a snare. "What of the white man?"

"Mix some dust into his water and I will make sure he drinks it," she said.

"He will be poisoned?" the brave grunted. "I could kill him quicker myself."

"Spirit Bear wants Hevo to kill him." Shifting her weight so she could curl up on top of Hevo while also giving the brave a generous view of her bare breasts, Namid said, "It will prove his loyalty to us before he rides on the next hunt."

Although the brave was disappointed that he wouldn't be allowed to kill Slocum, he seemed willing to take the orders. After one last look at the naked beauty coiled on top of Hevo, he departed and passed the orders along to the other guard waiting outside.

Once they stomped away, Namid quickly gathered up her clothes and pulled them on. "You must wait here," she whispered. "They will bring their water poisoned with Dreaming Dust and I will make it seem as if you are drinking it."

"I can still take good amounts of it," Hevo told her.

"I'll still try to spill more on your chin than what gets into your mouth." Now that she was dressed, she went to his feet and positioned the cut ropes so they draped across his ankles and the severed ends were tucked neatly beneath them. "That will have to do. Try not to move," she said while crawling around the post to do a similar job with the ropes around his wrists. Once they were wrapped around him, Hevo pressed his arms against the post to hold the ropes in place.

"When is this hunt supposed to happen?" he asked.

"Soon. The scouts have found the wagons that you and this other man have been trying to protect."

Hevo sat up with almost enough force to send his broken ropes flying through the air. When he spoke, it took every last bit of restraint to keep from raising his voice. "Are you sure?"

"Yes. The warriors are anxious to take those women and strip the wagons. Some even speak of taking the children and selling them as slaves." When Hevo tried to stand, she pushed him down again with one hand flat upon his chest. "You know as well as I that we cannot move too swiftly. There will only be one chance to stop them, and if we miss it, we will die along with those families."

"The dead ones will be the lucky ones." Hevo pulled in a deep breath and nodded. "But you are right. We cannot move too swiftly. We must be ready for when the time comes. I must get to John Slocum and free him before one of the braves takes it upon himself to kill him."

"They will not. I spoke the truth about Spirit Bear's request that you should kill the white man. He likes the idea of you pledging yourself to him again in this way."

"There is much that must be done," Hevo insisted. "We must get our weapons back. I will also need a chance to speak with my friend before the others come. We need to make sure—"

Namid silenced him with a kiss. "I will see to your friend. Give me some time and then make your way back to the cabin where he is being held. Be careful, my whirlwind. I do not want to lose you again."

18

Slocum was in the same spot as he'd been when Namid had taken Hevo away. When she returned, there was only one brave accompanying her.

"Looks like you had a good reunion," Slocum said. "I think I heard some of it not too long ago."

"Hevo was wrong to stray from the righteous path," she said. "I have come to give you a chance to follow that path as well."

"Oh, really? Are you going to make me an offer to join up with you?"

"Would you accept it?"

"Somehow I doubt that matters. I may be new around here, but I haven't seen a whole lot of faces that weren't Indian. Doesn't look like all of these men were pulled from the same tribe, but none of 'em are from Wichita, that's for damn sure."

"Spirit Bear sings of better times for this land and I believe those times are drawing close." Namid wore a water skin strapped over one shoulder. As she approached him, she removed the stopper and allowed some of its contents to trickle into one hand. "This is your first taste of the dreaming waters. Hevo will come soon to give you the rest. Then you will see the truth in Spirit Bear's words."

"What if I tell you to take that truth along with all those words and cram them sideways up Spirit Bear's ass?"

The brave stepped closer, holding a sawed-off shogun decorated with symbols painted along the barrel and feathers dangling from the stock.

"You would be wiser to hold your tongue and listen to what I say," she told him in a terse voice.

"Enough of this," the brave grunted as he thumbed back the hammers of his shotgun. "Spirit Bear wants this white man dead. After all the trouble he's caused, I think he will not care if I am the one to do it."

Hevo sat in his teepee, shifting nervously while trying to keep his ropes in place. The second brave that had dragged him from the cabin stood guard over him now, filling the entrance while holding the flap open using the tip of a large spear. Instead of a spearhead chiseled from rock, a blade that would have looked more at home on a Bowie knife had been lashed to the end of the shaft by several strips of rawhide.

Looking at the spear and then at the man who stood behind it, Hevo asked, "Which tribe did you belong to?"

"I am Sioux."

"Your weapon looks like no Sioux weapon I have ever seen."

"All that matters," the Sioux said, "is that my weapon is strong enough to kill what I put in front of it."

"Is that why you stand outside, afraid to be in the same space as a man who is bound to a post?"

"You do not speak like a warrior who wants to join the hunt with Spirit Bear's tribe."

Hevo chuckled under his breath. "You must have just come along. I rode with Spirit Bear and spilled many white men's blood. He must be desperate to fill his ranks if he is allowing a Sioux pretender to ride alongside his warriors."

Chanting was beginning to fill the camp again. Just being among the Dirt Swimmers and warriors again, Hevo could feel the rage that flowed through them all. Spirit Bear's camps never truly slept like a normal community. Some members would collapse and rest when they had to while others would dance and fight among themselves. As for Spirit Bear himself, none knew for certain if he ever slept. He would merely sit in his shelter and stare into his medicine fires. Because of the smoke that always hung in the air, it was difficult to tell when it was night or day. There was never any telling when the songs would start again and when hunters would be sent out. Now, it seemed, the drums were stirring the camp for another celebration. Soon after that, more blood would be spilled.

The Sioux hunched over and stepped into the teepee. His spear remained firmly in his grasp and the blade at its tip pushed against Hevo's chest until it broke the skin. "You call me a pretender? You think I am not a real warrior?"

Even as the end of the knife bored into his chest, Hevo looked up and said, "I think you're just another one of Spirit Bear's dogs who barks and runs whenever he is told."

The Sioux had been smiling confidently before. Hearing this wiped his smile away. He wasn't quite sure if he should be more angry or confused by the words coming from Hevo's spiteful mouth. "I could kill you."

"You could, but you won't." Smirking petulantly, Hevo added, "Spirit Bear has not snapped his fingers yet."

Baring his teeth like the dog Hevo had so recently mentioned, the Sioux gripped his spear and took another step into the teepee. The weight of his body was put behind the weapon as his arms tensed to drive it home. Half a second before the attack was made, Hevo twisted around the post so the knife slid across his chest and his shoulder bumped the spear to one side. The Sioux had already started ramming the weapon forward, and now that it had been deflected, he could only go farther into the teepee.

Hevo climbed to his feet. By the time the Sioux's spear had been driven into the dirt, Hevo had come all the way around the post to stand behind the warrior. He reached out to pluck a short-bladed knife from the scabbard hanging from the Sioux's belt. It was a traditional weapon with a carved stone blade and a handle made of bone that had most likely been passed down through the warrior's family. That bloodline would end when Hevo drove the blade in between the other man's ribs to puncture his organs. The Sioux tried to fight, but his strength was already leaving him.

"You chose the wrong side of this fight, my friend," Hevo whispered as he took hold of the spear and pulled it free from the soil. The Sioux tried to hang on to his weapon, but his grip was already failing him. Hevo set the spear aside in favor of the knife. "You have a killer's eyes. You would not have joined me."

The Sioux stood up as straight as he could. When Hevo pulled the knife from his side, blood poured from him like water from a punctured canteen. He opened his mouth to speak or cry out, only to be immediately silenced by Hevo's hand clamped over his face. Then, the bloody knife was dragged across his throat and he was lowered to the ground.

Hevo crouched above him, placing one hand upon the Sioux's twitching body just to make sure there was no more fight in him and watching the entrance flap for any reinforcements. For the moment, it seemed the teepee was entrusted to only one guard. Others would be coming, he knew.

The night was still young.

Slocum's challenge still hung in the air. The Indian with the shotgun stalked forward and came to a stop just inside the weapon's most effective range. That still put him outside of Slocum's kicking distance.

"What's the matter?" Slocum asked. "Big, bold spirit

warrior has to put a man down using a weapon that any woman could fire?"

But the Indian merely shook his head. "You are nothing to me, white man. The only purpose you serve is to bring money and gold to us so that we may take it."

"And here I thought you tribal folks were more concerned with the land."

"It is your people who value money so much. Good thing for us, your people do not care where that money comes from. I can take it from you and spend it as I please. Then I can take more until I can live better than your government would have me live on some patch of land that you do not want."

Squirming against the wall, Slocum ground his wrists against the nail that acted as a hook to keep his arms stretched above his head. Over the last several minutes, he'd been scraping at his own flesh to get a good flow of blood going. It wasn't the most ideal solution and it hurt like hell, but the blood got the ropes good and slick while the pain acted as a fire in his belly to keep him going. "How about you untie me and I'll give you a real fight?" he asked.

Once again, the Indian shook his head. "Don't want one," he replied. "Spirit Bear gives us plenty of white men to fight."

Namid rushed forward. "Come away from here! Spirit Bear will want to—"

The shotgunner cut her off by twisting around and slapping her face with the back of his hand. "Spirit Bear's a crazy old fool!"

The moment the shotgunner turned around, Slocum pushed away from the wall with all the power he could muster. He pulled his hands as if he had no doubt in his mind they would come along with him. The ropes dug into his bleeding wrists, sending a jolt of pain all the way down to his shoulders, and when he launched himself at the shotgunner, his hands slid through the bindings just as he'd hoped.

Still focusing on Namid, the shotgunner was slow to react and too proud to call for help. Perhaps her surprised yelp had been loud enough to mask the sound of Slocum's escape, or the impact of her hands and knees against the floorboards blended with his hurried footsteps. Either way, Slocum was able to close in on the shotgunner before the Indian knew what was coming.

Every instinct in Slocum's body told him to grab the shotgun and put it to use. That would most definitely bring plenty more warriors running so Slocum pounded a fist against the Indian's chin to loosen the other man's grip on the weapon.

Although Slocum started to take the shotgun away, the guard immediately tried to grab it back. That put the two men in a deadly tug-of-war when it came to fighting for control of the shotgun. Slocum had one hand near the trigger and another at the base of the barrel. The Indian's were just above the trigger and at the end of the barrel.

Both men had a chance at getting a finger to the trigger and would suffer burnt hands if the gun went off.

When one tried to pull the weapon closer, the other dragged it in another direction.

Finally, Slocum pivoted his body to the right. When the Indian countered by leaning against him, Slocum switched directions and pulled the guard in closer while slamming his left elbow around to knock against his ear. It wasn't a powerful blow, but it caused the bigger man to stagger. The Indian shook it off in less than a second and renewed his attempts to retrieve his weapon with even more vigor.

Slocum pulled the weapon in, bringing the other man less than an inch toward him in the process. Then, he snapped his right leg up and out to pound his knee into the brave's stomach. A few inches lower and he would have hit an even more sensitive spot. Judging by the snarl coming from the Indian's throat, however, that may have just incensed the shotgunner further.

Grunting with an exhale, the Indian absorbed the blow fairly well. He responded by pulling the shotgun back and bringing Slocum in to receive a knee of his own. He thumped his leg into Slocum's midsection once and again in quick succession. The first hit knocked some wind from Slocum's lungs. The second made him unsteady on his feet. When he was too weak to do anything before the third blow came, Slocum began to wonder if he wouldn't have been better off hanging from a nail in the wall like a crooked picture frame.

Suddenly, the Indian leaned back. His face twisted into an angry mask that flushed with color. When he tried to speak, all he could get out was a hoarse gurgling sound. That's when Slocum noticed the thin arm wrapped around the guard's neck from behind. He took advantage of the opening that had been created for him by pushing the shotgun out and up. Even with his hands wrapped around the weapon, the Indian couldn't keep its barrel from being jammed beneath his chin.

"All right, big man," Slocum grunted. "You'd best get real still before I yank this trigger."

The Indian's eyes were already wide, but they became even more so when he looked down at that shotgun. His hand was still near the top of the trigger assembly, but Slocum's was much closer. Suddenly tentative to draw another breath for fear of getting his brains splattered onto the ceiling of the cabin, the Indian nodded slowly while Namid continued to dangle from the back of his neck. Despite all of that, he refused to take his hands completely off the weapon.

"You can let go of him now, little lady," Slocum said.

Her arm relaxed, allowing her to slide along the large man's back and land on her feet.

Slocum kept his eyes on the guard as he told her, "Back away."

She did and immediately went to the cabin's door.

"Looks like I've got the upper hand here," Slocum said

to the man in front of him. "That is, unless you'd like to keep trying to wrestle this shotgun from me?"

"If I let go, you will shoot me anyway."

"You might have a point there." Slocum cracked the barrel against his chin and followed up with a kick to the Indian's stomach. This time, his knee found its exact mark, landing in the spot needed to double the other man over.

Slocum's biggest concern was to keep from pulling the shotgun's trigger. He kept his finger poised over it without setting the gun off. As soon as the other man's grip went slack, he took the shotgun away and swung the stock around to connect with the Indian's temple. By the time the guard landed heavily on the floor, Slocum was wheezing.

"That was even harder than I was expecting," he said. "Get over here before I decide to fire this gun after all."

Namid didn't move from the doorway. "I came to help you."

"That doesn't mean I trust you all the way. Now get over here."

She stepped away from the door, only to go to the window. "The others are preparing for a hunt. They mean to go after the rest of your wagons."

"Where's Hevo?"

"He is close."

Slocum searched the Indian he'd knocked cold, but didn't find much more than a few spare shotgun shells in a pouch hanging from his belt. Stuffing the shells into his pocket, he took the shotgun and went to the window. "Where are our weapons?"

"They will probably be with the rest of the guns, but there isn't enough time to get them. Spirit Bear will be coming."

"And I don't aim to be here when he arrives. Take me to the weapons."

She shook her head, even when she saw Slocum pointing the shotgun at her. "I tried to help you get away," she said. "I have made it so Hevo can also escape. The entire camp is preparing for war. I cannot get to your weapons, and even if I did, we would not make it to that part of the camp without being seen. Someone will be coming for you any moment now. If you want to escape with your life, you must go now! You are to be killed before the hunt," she said. "Even now, I am supposed to help with preparations."

Slocum looked through the window, taking note of the increased amount of activity throughout the rest of the camp. From the cabin, he could see a good portion of the settlement, including a growing number of women in attire similar to Namid's, scurrying among the waist-high posts topped with large wooden bowls and dented brass lanterns. "Where is Hevo being kept?"

"Straight across from here in one of the small teepees near the edge of camp."

"Never mind," Slocum said. "Already found him." Hevo emerged from one of the teepees and crept toward the trees, moving like another one of the shadows. Because the others in the camp were so busy with their own tasks, they did not notice him.

"Spirit Bear will be singing soon," she told Slocum. "And when he does, the warriors will gather to fight the war he has put in front of them."

"They won't want to fight once things swing too far in the wrong direction," Slocum replied.

"You do not know that."

"I may not have seen every last one of these men, but the ones I have seen are no fanatics. That one back there," he said while nodding toward the unconscious guard, "was more concerned with saving his own skin than putting me down. That's the sign of a common, greedy brute. If that man was truly sworn to Spirit Bear like the crazed killers they're supposed to be, he would have come at me a lot harder whether there was a gun pointed at him or not. Trust me. I've looked into the eyes of crazy men and I've fought fanatics. That man down there wasn't either one of those."

"But there are plenty who would follow Spirit Bear to the grave," Namid swore.

"I'll grant you that much. But that makes it even easier for me to put an end to this."

"Just you?"

"So far, that's about all I got."

Namid's head hung low. "And what about Hevo?" she asked. "He trusts you. Otherwise he would not have brought you here to stand with him against Spirit Bear. You should trust him as well. It will be hard enough for you two to get away from here together. Apart, you would stand no chance."

"I intend on doing a hell of a lot more than just get away from here," Slocum said.

19

Activity within the camp built to a furor. More and more warriors visited a large tent at the other end of the clearing and emerged carrying rifles, spears, knives, or bows. Other men prepared horses to be ridden, and women furiously worked to apply a fresh coat of leaves to cloaks that were given to the Dirt Swimmers. Food was handed out and drums began to sound, all while Hevo worked his way toward the cabin.

Slocum watched intently from his window. He kept the shotgun ready so he could fire at the guard if he should stir, and he kept his muscles tensed in case he needed to lunge for the woman, who grew more impatient with every second that passed. But Namid didn't seem to be interested in running. She barely made a sound as she stood in the doorway, nodding to the occasional Indian who would look in her direction. Slocum watched for a hint that she might be passing some sort of signal to the others, even though he wasn't sure what he could do to stop her or what options he might have if she did call for help. Even those few who nodded back to Namid were too busy to do much else.

After what couldn't have been more than a few minutes, Hevo crept around the perimeter of the camp to the back of the cabin. First chance he got, he darted to the cabin's only door and rushed inside, where Namid greeted him with open arms.

"I should have stayed with you," she said. "I should never have left you."

"You did plenty," Hevo replied. As he stroked her hair, he looked over at Slocum.

Still pointing the shotgun toward the door, Slocum said, "You two sure seem a lot friendlier."

"She has turned against Spirit Bear as I have," Hevo told him. "She just could not get away when I did."

"Now there's a cryin' shame."

"This is a tangled mess, John," Hevo sighed. "All I can offer you is my word that she can be trusted."

Slocum maintained a solid poker face as he thought a few things over. First of all, Hevo had proven himself more often than not. More than anything else, Slocum preferred to judge another man based on his actions. Hevo had stood tall when things had gotten rough. He'd waded into battle when the wagons were being attacked, and when he had the opportunity to run now, he'd come back to the cabin for Namid. Mistakes may have been made, but Slocum could relate to making much worse mistakes where women were concerned.

As far as that woman was concerned, Slocum knew even less. Since he was going to be discovered sooner or later if he stayed in one spot, it didn't seem bad to risk it now. A mess was a mess, and he was already in this one up to his ears.

"So you want out of here?" Slocum asked her.

Namid looked at Hevo, who offered her nothing in the way of any hint as to how he wanted her to answer. She looked at Slocum and nodded. "I am only here because I cannot leave. If I was to slip away in the night, I would be found. What they would do to me after that would be worse than death."

"So that was all an act before?"

"I had to get Hevo alone," she explained.

"She will come with us, John," Hevo said. "If you will not allow her to come with us, then I will take her on my own."

"She can come with us," Slocum sighed while taking another gander out the window. "In fact, I think she can be a big help in getting us away from this madhouse."

"I cannot get to your weapons," she insisted.

"I'm not worried about that anymore. There's more than enough weapons out there for us to shoot our way out of this place, into another place, into a fort, and out of there as well. My concern is getting the ball rolling and I think there might be a real easy way to get that part done."

Hevo had taken a spot near the window and was now looking outside with one eye so he only exposed a sliver of himself to the rest of the camp. "I forgot what it was like to be here," he said almost to himself. "There is no rest. No time for meals. Everyone works on Spirit Bear's schedule and that man does not even let the sun or moon tell him when to lay his head down."

"Spirit Bear rarely sleeps anymore," Namid said. "He meditates and chants, all while smoking his own dust or drinking his potions."

Turning to her, Slocum said, "He can't be the only one who mixes that stuff. Considering how much dust gets burned, thrown around, and mixed into food or water, he wouldn't have time for much else."

She lowered her head and crossed her arms as if to cocoon herself. "I have helped with the mixtures. All of the women have. It is what we do to survive. One of the many things for which I am ashamed."

Hevo went to her right away and said, "You should not be ashamed."

"It is because of the Dreaming Dust that Spirit Bear turns his prisoners into workers and killers. It is the dust that allows the hunts to go on. I was even here for some time because of it. That dust has robbed me of memories and put nightmares in their place."

"That is over," Hevo said while shaking her as if to snap her out of those nightmares and make certain he was heard. In his own language, he added, *"From this day onward, that nightmare is over. Do you understand me?"*

She took comfort by responding in her native tongue. *"I understand. I will never be able to make up for what I did to you."* Looking toward Slocum, she added, *"What I did to others who were innocent."*

"We can start by putting an end to this. That is why John and I are here."

"I know," she said while nodding. Drawing a deep breath, she nodded again with more conviction.

"You two done sweet talking over there?" Slocum asked.

"We have talked enough," Hevo replied. "There is no more time for it."

"I agree. Will you be ready to help?"

"I want to help also," Namid said.

"Good," Slocum replied. "Because I was talking to you in the first place. What can you tell me about that Dreaming Dust?"

"It is similar to peyote and other medicines used by my tribe's shaman. Many tribes use something like it as well. But Spirit Bear's mixture is more potent. It is more like the opium used in parlors where men pay to dream their days away."

"I guessed as much," Slocum said. "But I've smelled opium and I've smelled peyote. This is something else. Do you know how to mix it up so it's something more?"

Namid made a face that reflected how badly that notion sat within her. "What do you mean . . . more?"

As Slocum explained what he had in mind, Namid's

expression shifted to something much brighter. When he finished and asked, "So do you think you could pull that off?" she was already nodding.

"We won't have much time," he said.

Namid rushed past both men and glanced outside. "I will not need much time, but I must go now before it is too late to do what you ask."

"How long before we know you got it right?"

"Maybe a minute or two. Not much longer than that. You must be prepared for when my job is done. Even you," she said to Hevo. "I fear this may be too much for your friend, but I wouldn't want to risk you as well."

Slocum rolled his eyes at suddenly being talked about like he was some stray dog that just happened to be standing in the corner.

"I will be fine," Hevo assured her. "Do not think about us while doing your part. Just do what you must so that we may put an end to this. When we are through, we will be free." Turning to Slocum as a last-ditch effort to make him feel like he was still a part of the conversation, he added, "All of us."

"No need to convince me," Slocum said as he approached Namid so he could gently usher her toward the door before she and Hevo got sentimental again. "It was my idea, remember?"

"Of course," she said before taking a deep breath. Apart from steeling her for what was to come, that breath set off a change that brought Namid right back to the cold-hearted exterior she'd worn when Slocum had first laid eyes on her. The mask slid into place and she was careful not to look at either of the men when she strode out of the cabin.

Watching her through the window, Slocum had to duck out of sight as some of the preparing warriors outside took notice of her and looked toward the cabin. Plastering his back against the wall beside the window, he whispered, "You think she can pull this off?"

"She has convinced them she is still following Spirit Bear."

"No, I mean what I asked her to do. Do you think she can get that done? Because if it doesn't go off just right, we could be in a whole world of hurt."

Hevo stood away from the window with his arms crossed over his chest. His eyes were pointed straight ahead as if he could see straight through the cabin wall. "She will do her part. We must do ours."

"Yeah, and that brings us to a whole new set of problems." Slocum peeled his shirt off and took it to a corner so he could have his back to a wall and get a good view of the rest of the cabin without being too close to the door or window. "We've got a shotgun and some shells, but that's about it."

"You said we could get weapons. Spirit Bear may have an addled mind, but his men know how to arm themselves."

Slocum trapped his shirt under the heel of one boot and pulled a sleeve until it ripped off. "Which is another thing. I haven't even met this Spirit Bear fellow."

"You have seen what he does," Hevo said through a heavy scowl. "Isn't that enough to judge him?"

"Not if I'm dropping a death sentence onto him." He shifted his shirt so the other sleeve was under his boot.

"Are you having second thoughts?" Hevo asked.

"No, I'm just mulling over the thoughts I do have. What I said before is true. We're in this too deep to get out quietly now. And even if we could get away from here, Ed and the others in those wagons would still be in danger. Nope," he grunted while ripping another strip of thick cotton from his shirt, "we go forward just as planned."

When Hevo grinned, it was an odd sight. Considering their circumstances, having something else strike Slocum as odd was saying quite a bit. "This is a good plan, John. Otherwise, I would not have allowed my Star Dancer to be a part of it."

"Only problem with this plan is that if it goes wrong, it'll go wrong in a real big way."

"Then it must not go wrong."

Slocum didn't have anything to say to that. The sound of his ripping shirt tore through the cabin as the drums outside grew louder.

20

Slocum and Hevo didn't have much else to do by way of preparation. Now was the time when Namid proved herself, and if she failed or decided she truly did belong with Spirit Bear, the drums that were now pounding in a rhythmic frenzy would most likely be the last music that Slocum heard. He had faith in his plan. He only wished he'd had more than a few minutes to put the plan together.

"You seem nervous, John," Hevo said. While Slocum had been making his preparations and mulling things over, the Cheyenne had been dipping his fingers into mud from the floor mixed with blood from his wounds to make war paint, which he used to trace lines on his cheeks, forearms, and chest.

Slocum finished knotting a few strips of his shirt together, sniffed it, and winced. "And you don't look nervous. That means you might be even crazier than those men outside."

"I have faith in our cause. Even if we fall in this fight, we will have died in a righteous manner."

"Yeah, well, let's try not to die at all," Slocum said while tossing over the strips he'd knotted together. "That way we can tell folks personally how righteous we are."

Hevo chuckled and caught the shredded pieces of shirt. "You are no boasting rooster like the man Josiah, who stays behind to squawk to the women and children within those wagons."

"Josiah. I damn near forgot about him." Picking up another couple strips of fabric that had been knotted and soaked with as much water as he could sop up from the floor and windowsill, Slocum tied the strips together. Like the piece he'd made for Hevo, his strip was the length of a shirt-sleeve with several other strips of cotton in layers. He smelled the fabric and winced at the pungent mixture of mold, dirt, and even dung that had been left behind by some-thing that had lived up in the cabin's rafters. "I hope that loudmouthed old man is doing all right."

"Have faith, John Slocum." Lifting his head, Hevo nod-ded at the subtle shift in drumbeats.

"Is Spirit Bear about to make his speech?" Slocum asked. Hevo nodded.

"About damn time." With that, Slocum placed the foul-smelling rags across the lower portion of his face and tied the ends tightly in back of his head.

Hevo did the same with his own makeshift mask, chant-ing a song in a low, growling voice while the Indians in the camp struck up a tune of their own.

Slocum could barely smell the cotton through the mess he'd smeared into the fabric. When the odor of the animal dung washed down his throat, he longed for the pungent stench of body odor or any number of things that could have been in the shirt before. Cold air blew through the cabin, stinging his chest like a set of icy nails dragging through his flesh.

Outside, the drums played and women made their rounds to the bowls and lanterns to add a granular mixture from bags they carried. One of those women was Namid and she went about her task without casting more than half a side-ways glance at the cabin where Hevo and Slocum were hiding. Seconds after the mixture was added to the bowls, it was lit by torches. Lanterns flared as dust was added to the kerosene within them and the remaining dust carried by the women was cast into a large fire that had been built in the middle of camp. As soon as dark green smoke billowed from the flames, Spirit Bear emerged from the largest tent.

Decked out in his skins and wearing a headpiece made from the hollowed skull of his namesake, Spirit Bear looked more like a shape-shifting animal from Indian legend than any sort of man. He shook his staff, extended both arms toward the growing cloud of smoke, and began to speak in a powerful, wavering voice.

"What's he saying?" Slocum asked.

Hevo watched intently, translating as if he was speaking from memory. "Tonight, we hunt!" he said. "Tonight we slaughter the white travelers who would disgrace our lands with their boots."

At first, the answers from the warriors and Dirt Swimmers gathered around the fire were given as if they'd been well rehearsed. As Spirit Bear continued, the responses became wilder.

"Tonight we slaughter demons dressed in the skins of men!" Hevo translated.

The men near the fire threw their hands up and howled as if they fully intended to shred their throats with the effort. Spirit Bear went on, trembling with emotion.

"Do not see them as anything but the demons they are!" Spirit Bear continued. "Some may be small and some may have fairer skin, but they are all foul demons!"

Now the men on the periphery of the camp started shouting. They were closest to the wooden bowls that burned with the Dreaming Dust. Some fired their guns in the air while others began flailing so powerfully that they knocked into each other. Random fights broke out among them and a few looked around in a panic before running toward the hills, leaving the camp behind altogether.

Spirit Bear chanted, but none of the others chanted back. He shook his staff and chanted louder, which only seemed to create more of a panic among the men, who now ran in a frenzy of flailing arms and thrashing legs.

"Looks like a good time to join the dance," Slocum said. He ran through the door and exploded from the cabin with Hevo following closely behind. The first time Slocum passed through a cloud of the acrid smoke, he held his breath beneath the mask he'd created. The smoke sung his eyes, causing tears to flow and a painful ache to take root at his temples. Whatever he was feeling, however, the men who breathed it in directly were feeling a whole lot worse.

Three men closest to the cabin saw Slocum and Hevo charge out and immediately turned their backs to them. Slocum had been expecting resistance right away, but hadn't expected to see such well-armed braves scamper away like children who'd just seen a strange shadow in the corner of their bedroom. Hevo shifted his focus to a bare-chested warrior holding a tomahawk in one hand and a rifle in the other. Although the warrior held his ground, he cowered when Hevo hunched over and snarled like a wolf that had been raised in the lowest regions of hell.

The warrior tried to turn tail, but Hevo was already upon him. He snatched the tomahawk away and swung it viciously across the warrior's throat. Even when the warrior dropped, his arms and legs thrashed wildly as if he was still trying to run away. Hevo knocked him out with a swift kick to the chin and then scooped up the warrior's rifle.

Slocum emptied both barrels of his shotgun at a pair of warriors who rushed at him. Although his mask was doing a good job of filtering out the Dreaming Dust, it was making his hands shake so hard that he dropped the spare shells he meant to use to reload the shotgun. He found time to reload, simply because the warriors in his vicinity were too busy either fighting each other or bolting into the hills surrounding the camp to worry about him. When the shotgun shells were spent, Slocum found a few rifles that had been cast away by warriors too intent on escaping whatever visions they were seeing. He took one rifle and slung it across his back before picking up a Spencer model that had been decorated with tribal charms and feathers.

All this time, Spirit Bear continued to chant. He stood his ground in the thick of the smoke, wailing to the sky above and stomping the ground in steps that became heavier and faster with each second that passed.

Some of the warriors that Slocum and Hevo found next still had some fight left in them. Whatever Namid had done to the Dreaming Dust made it difficult even for the most focused warriors to concentrate long enough to use their weapons. The ones who bore firearms couldn't see straight enough to hit the broad side of a barn. Any shots they fired either hissed several yards over Slocum's head or clipped one of the other painted braves and spun them around like broken marionettes.

Slocum kept his breaths shallow whenever possible. He focused on the putrid tastes and smells of the mask he'd crafted, hoping that some of the tangy scents he detected weren't from wisps of the modified dust seeping through the protective layers. Taking in some of the smoke was unavoidable, however. Slocum's vision began to blur and shadows started writhing as if they had lives of their own. Noises became a slurred mess within his ears until his own footsteps sounded like a snarling voice. By the time he'd fought his way to Spirit Bear, Slocum pitied the crazed wretches who'd gotten a real taste of the altered smoke.

"You . . . are . . . *demons!*" Spirit Bear hollered in slurred English. His eyes were wide beneath the bear skin hood, and his muscles trembled beneath his cloak. "White demons come to . . . eat my *soul!*"

"Just one white man," Slocum replied.

Hevo yelped like a coyote as he shoved aside a pair of staggering warriors and hurdled a group of Dirt Swimmers who clawed at the ground in an effort to live up to their name. His eyes were so wide and his voice so powerful that Slocum wondered if too much of the poisoned dust had gotten into his lungs. Spirit Bear looked at the Cheyenne warrior and dropped to his knees to chant crazily as Hevo rushed toward him. When he arrived, Hevo grabbed hold of Spirit Bear's headdress, raised his tomahawk, and then swung it with a mighty war cry. Although he stopped short of burying the blade into Spirit Bear's neck, he lifted the headdress up and wailed as if he'd just slain the most fearsome beast the prairie had ever seen. He continued to shout as he kicked Spirit Bear over and held him down with that foot.

Many of the Indians in the immediate vicinity didn't notice the performance right away. But when one of the warriors caught sight of Hevo standing over Spirit Bear, the man screamed. His voice caught the ear of others and silence worked its way through the camp like ripples in water.

Hevo stood with his prize in hand, glaring at any eye that dared to look in his direction.

Sensing a fear that was powerful enough to make the air feel like a taut bowstring, Slocum fired his rifle and shouted his own string of nonsense words. Any other time, the display may have been laughable. To the men who'd been affected by the smoke Namid had poisoned, Slocum may as well have been the devil himself.

More warriors ran away.

The ones who attempted to fire at Slocum and Hevo didn't come anywhere close to hitting them. All Slocum had to do was fire a shot in their general direction to send that group running like scalded dogs.

Dirt Swimmers cast their netted cloaks aside and bolted from the camp.

Before long, Slocum, Hevo, and less than half a dozen

others were all that remained. Those others were either sprawled unconscious on the ground or babbling like lunatics in an asylum.

The smoke was clearing. Hevo kicked Spirit Bear aside and walked toward the largest tent. A woman cried inside and he could not get to her fast enough.

Slocum stooped down to prop Spirit Bear up to a seated position. Once his skins were off and his ceremonial trappings had been stripped, Spirit Bear was nothing more than an old man with wide, clouded eyes. His cracked lips moved to form words that could not be heard. His hands trembled and panicked breaths caused his sunken chest to quake beneath filthy undergarments that most likely hadn't been washed for months.

"Whatever you were trying to do," Slocum told him, "it's over. You're through with your damn war. You hear me?"

Spirit Bear kept babbling his silent chant. Without an army to follow him and without anyone to listen to his big talk, he was exposed for what he truly was: a feeble, yammering old man. Slocum brought him to his feet and shoved him toward the livery that had been set up beneath a makeshift shelter.

By the time Spirit Bear was tied up and tossed over the back of a horse, Hevo was escorting Namid from the big tent. She was sobbing and rubbing her eyes. Hevo comforted her in their native language, but wouldn't be heard for some time. Even so, he continued to try and calm her down as they rode into the hills.

They retraced their steps across the prairie. Along the way, they crossed paths with a few crazed Indians who were still feeling the effects of the Dreaming Dust. The ones that weren't easily knocked out and tied up were convinced to run away by a few loud noises.

The following day, as they continued to ride, a few more Indians tracked them down. Slocum and Hevo had been watching for stubborn ones like that and managed to gun them down before they got close enough to do any damage. The fights were as short as they were one-sided.

"They are just animals," Namid said. "Without Spirit Bear to guide them or bring them together, those men are nothing but wild dogs."

"Looks that way," Slocum said. "Soon as I get to an Army post or even a town with a telegraph, I can send word out to keep a lookout for them."

"Considering all the suffering Spirit Bear has caused," Hevo said while looking at the old man still tied up and draped across a saddle, "there will be plenty of white men who are more than willing to begin a hunt of their own. For once, I cannot blame them. Men like these make all tribes look like savages."

"Well, there are plenty of palefaces out and about who make handsome fellas like me look just as bad," Slocum said. "I'm just glad we were able to come out of that camp in one piece. Speaking of which," he added while looking over to Namid, "what on earth did you do to that dust?"

Namid had recovered from her dose of the smoke, but had been withdrawn ever since. "I did as you asked. I made it . . . more."

"What was the ingredient that caused all of that insanity?" Slocum asked.

"I do not know and I do not want to know. Spirit Bear showed the women how to mix the Dreaming Dust and he gave us the ingredients. He showed us the powders we needed to handle most carefully and those are what I put into the smoke when I mixed it for the last time. I put more than we should have used for three doses. Maybe more."

"You convinced all the women to help you?"

She nodded. "All of us were in our own nightmares at the hands of those killers. When it came time for it to end, I knew the others would want to help."

"Hopefully nobody else stumbles upon that stuff," Slocum said.

"They won't," Namid told him. "We burned it all. Some of those killers who breathed in so much of it may never wake up from their nightmare."

Slocum wasn't about to pity the warriors and Dirt Swimmers who'd raided innocent wagon trains and killed good folks to steal their belongings, but when he thought about the madness that would grip them for the foreseeable future, he came awfully close.

21

When Slocum approached the spot outside of the town where the wagons had been left, he was nearly shot by an overly anxious Josiah. As it turned out, the near-miss was the most excitement the group had had since Slocum and Hevo had struck out on their own. The entire group was more than ready to get moving, and even though there was barely enough daylight for the wagons to travel a few miles, they did so in high spirits.

Hevo and Namid bade their farewells almost immediately. Their lands were to the northeast, and they were anxious to get back to them. Even so, the McCauley children wouldn't let them go before they'd had a chance to tell Namid how beautiful her flowing hair was. James Wilcox smiled at her and wouldn't say a word. It seemed the young boy was taken with her as well.

Despite his obligations to remain with the wagons, Slocum felt it more important to deal with Spirit Bear once and for all. There was an Army supply post a day's ride to the northwest, and he took the old man there before any of his more persistent followers took it upon themselves to find him on their own. Every step of the way, Spirit Bear muttered and chanted. Just when it seemed the old man had found a soothing melody, he would shift into a heated tirade about the death of all white men. For the last stretch of trail leading to the outpost, Slocum stuffed a bandanna in Spirit Bear's mouth so he could ride in peace.

The man who took custody of Spirit Bear was a sergeant named Owen Teales. He didn't seem to know what to do with Spirit Bear until Slocum explained that the old man was behind the recent attacks scattered across this and many other territories.

"Just take some men to his camp in the hills," Slocum told the young sergeant. "Be sure to keep your guard up, though. There'll be more redskins than you'll know what to do with in those parts."

Feeling he might be able to impress his superiors, Sergeant Teales agreed to send a cavalry unit to Spirit Bear's camp in the hills. Slocum gave him directions, made sure Spirit Bear was locked up, and headed out in the morning to meet up with the wagons. Normally, pointing a group of Indian hunters toward a cluster of targets wouldn't set well with Slocum. Having met those particular targets on more than one occasion, however, he found it fitting that those crazed killers and thieves meet their end at the hands of a bunch of well-armed palefaces.

Once he'd reunited with the wagon train, Slocum rode with them all the way into Colorado. It was a quiet trip, marred only by a few tough river crossings, during which they lost a pair of horses and busted a wheel. Upon arriving at the portion of the Rockies where Ed's mining claims were, the group disbanded to begin their new lives.

"Stay with us, John," Theresa said when she'd carried her first armload of possessions into an old log cabin that was to be her and James's new home. "At least for a little while."

"That's not part of the deal," he replied. "I was only paid

to get you here." When she scowled at him, Slocum grinned and kissed her on the cheek. "I'll check in on you two when I come along to collect my percentage of that claim."

She pulled him close and whispered, "How about staying until the morning? I'd love to have one more night with you."

Slocum felt a pull toward the open trail, but he wasn't about to refuse a lady.

Watch for

SLOCUM AND THE GRIZZLY FLATS KILLERS

408th novel in the exciting SLOCUM series
from Jove

Coming in February!

2794

DON'T MISS A YEAR OF

Slocum Giant
by
Jake Logan

penguin.com/actionwesterns

M457AS0812